Adams Didn't Want To Speak Of The Past, Or Even The Future.

He didn't want to think of anything but Eden. "You are beautiful."

"I'm not really beautiful, Adams. I'm only Eden, and once just one of the guys."

"Sweetheart—" his drawl was unconsciously seductive "—it's been a long time since you were one of the guys."

At her look of surprise, Adams's first instinct was to fold her in his arms, to show her in ways words never could that she was beautiful. So beautiful the memory of her moonlit image had been strength and solace for a lonely man in his worst days.

He'd known beautiful women. But never in love. Never in tenderness. And no matter how he'd searched, none had been Eden.

Now she was here, only a forbidden touch away....

* * *

Men of Belle Terre:
Honorable, loyal...and destined for love.

Dear Reader,

Silhouette is celebrating our 20th anniversary in 2000, and the latest powerful, passionate, provocative love stories from Silhouette Desire are as hot as that steamy summer weather!

For August's MAN OF THE MONTH, the fabulous BJ James begins her brand-new miniseries, MEN OF BELLE TERRE. In *The Return of Adams Cade*, a self-made millionaire returns home to find redemption in the arms of his first love.

Beloved author Cait London delivers another knockout in THE TALLCHIEFS miniseries with *Tallchief: The Homecoming*, also part of the highly sensual Desire promotion BODY & SOUL. And Desire is proud to present *Bride of Fortune* by Leanne Banks, the launch title of FORTUNE'S CHILDREN: THE GROOMS, another exciting spin-off of the bestselling Silhouette FORTUNE'S CHILDREN continuity miniseries.

BACHELOR BATTALION marches on with Maureen Child's *The Last Santini Virgin*, in which a military man's passion for a feisty virgin weakens his resolve not to marry. *In Name Only* is how a sexy rodeo cowboy agrees to temporarily wed a pregnant preacher's daughter in the second book of Peggy Moreland's miniseries TEXAS GROOMS. And Christy Lockhart reconciles a once-married couple who are stranded together in a wintry cabin during *One Snowbound Weekend....*

So indulge yourself by purchasing all six of these summer delights from Silhouette Desire...and read them in air-conditioned comfort.

Enjoy!

Joan Marlow Golan

Joan Marlow Golan
Senior Editor, Silhouette Desire

Please address questions and book requests to:
Silhouette Reader Service
U.S.: 3010 Walden Ave., P.O. Box 1325, Buffalo, NY 14269
Canadian: P.O. Box 609, Fort Erie, Ont. L2A 5X3

The Return of Adams Cade

BJ JAMES

Published by Silhouette Books
America's Publisher of Contemporary Romance

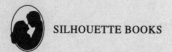

SILHOUETTE BOOKS

ISBN 0-373-76309-3

THE RETURN OF ADAMS CADE

Copyright © 2000 by BJ James

This edition published by arrangement with Harlequin Books S.A.

® and TM are trademarks of Harlequin Books S.A., used under license.
Trademarks indicated with ® are registered in the United States Patent
and Trademark Office, the Canadian Trade Marks Office and in other
countries.

Visit Silhouette at www.eHarlequin.com

Printed in U.S.A.

Books by BJ James

Silhouette Desire

The Sound of Goodbye #332
Twice in a Lifetime #396
Shiloh's Promise #529
Winter Morning #595
Slade's Woman #672
A Step Away #692
Tears of the Rose #709
*The Man with the
   Midnight Eyes* #751
Pride and Promises #789
Another Time, Another Place #823
The Hand of an Angel #844
*Heart of the Hunter #945
*The Saint of Bourbon Street #951
*A Wolf in the Desert #956
†Whispers in the Dark #1081
†Journey's End #1106
†Night Music #1286
‡The Return of Adams Cade #1309

Silhouette Intimate Moments

Broken Spurs #733

Silhouette Books

World's Most Eligible Bachelors
†*Agent of the Black Watch*

*Men of the Black Watch
†The Black Watch
‡Men of Belle Terre

BJ JAMES's

first book for Silhouette Desire was published in February 1987. Her second Desire novel garnered for BJ a second Maggie, the coveted award of the Georgia Romance Writers. Through the years there have been other awards and nominations for awards, including, from *Romantic Times Magazine,* Reviewer's Choice, Career Achievement, Best Desire and Best Series Romance of the Year. In that time, her books have appeared regularly on a number of bestseller lists, among them Waldenbooks and *USA Today.*

On a personal note, BJ and her physician husband have three sons and two grandsons. While her address reads Mooresboro, this is only the origin of a mail route passing through the countryside. A small village set in the foothills of western North Carolina is her home.

FOREWORD

In the coastal Lowcountry of South Carolina, where the fresh waters of winding rivers flow into the sea, there is an Eden of unmatched wonders. In this mix of waters and along the shores by which they carve their paths, life is rich and varied. The land is one of uncommon contrasts, with sandy, sea-swept beaches, mysterious swamps, teeming marshes bounded by ancient maritime forests. And a multitude of creatures abide in each.

In this realm of palms and palmettos, estuaries and rivers, shaded by towering live oaks draped in ghostly Spanish moss, lies Belle Terre. Like an exquisite pearl set among emeralds and sapphires, with its name the small, antebellum city describes its province. As it describes itself.

Belle Terre, beautiful land. A beautiful city.

A very proper, very elegant, beautiful city. A gift for the soul. An exquisite mélange for the senses. With ancient and grand structures in varying states of repair and disrepair set along tree-lined, cobbled streets. With narrow, gated gardens lush with such greenery as resurrection and cinnamon ferns. And all of it wrapped in the lingering scent of camellias, azaleas, jessamine and magnolias.

Steeped in an aura of history, its culture and customs influenced by plantations that once abounded in the Lowcountry, as it clings to its past Belle Terre is a province of contradictions. Within its society one will find arrogance abiding with humility, cruelty with kindness, insolence with gentility, honor with depravity, and hatred with love.

As ever when the senses are whetted and emotions untamed, in Belle Terre there will be passion, romance and scandal.

Prologue

"Yes, sir, the controlling interest in the company is mine. No, sir, it isn't for sale." The expected acknowledgment was spoken softly. The rejection was delivered in courteous respect.

But not one man among the phalanx of powerful corporate elders mistook the softness, the respect or the courtesy. Men such as those seated in the subtly but flawlessly appointed office had not come unprepared. Each executive who sat so coolly beneath the steady gaze knew this much younger man was a southerner of good family, born and raised on an historic plantation in coastal South Carolina. Each knew he was a superb analyst and engineer for offshore oil rigs; an innovative, intuitive inventor, an astute investor, a canny businessman.

He was Adams Cade, at the relatively young age of thirty-seven the most promising young intellect of the modern business world. An exile from home and family. A convicted felon.

It was for the first this corporate board had come calling. For the latter that none misjudged gentle courtesies as weakness.

"Adams...if I may call you Adams?" Jacob Helms rose confidently from his seat. A tall, thin man, immaculately tailored, his every move was patrician, every word concise. "I realize Cade Enterprises has not been and will not be offered for sale."

Pausing, his faded stare locked with the unwavering silver-brown regard. Remembering another daring young lion challenging the old guard long ago, he almost smiled. "For that reason, we've come offering a different opportunity."

After a moment spent inspecting a wall hung with a mélange of superb paintings and yellowing photos, Jacob Helms continued, "We propose a meeting of the minds, an alliance, so to speak." A brow arched, Helms' head cocked in Adams Cade's direction. "The first time you've heard that, I wager."

Adams' expression was noncommittal. "Why?"

The question brought Jacob Helms up short. Peering over gold-rimmed glasses, he asked haughtily, "Why haven't you heard this proposal before?"

"No, sir, why am I hearing it now?" With a look at the men who waited to witness their leader's prowess, he added, "Why with the board of Helms, Helms, and Helms in tow?"

Helms paced, then turned with the grace of a ballet master giving his best performance for a new disciple. "Why, indeed."

Adams leaned back in his seat, an audience of one,

waiting for the curtain to lift over the real show. "Indeed."

"The answer is simple. Because we can offer the perfect deal. An alliance with a company offering services and products that mesh with your own." Hesitating, the venerable blue blood looked about him. "And because we've come offering millions."

A sweeping gesture indicated the small, uniquely efficient operation of Cade Enterprises, visible beyond a wall of windows. "Tens of millions."

"Why?" Adams' expression didn't change. "For what?"

"For whom." Helms corrected, his voice theatrical, as he moved in for the coup. "For John Quincy Adams Cade, eldest son of Caesar Augustus Cade. Scion of an elite family of South Carolina's low country. For you, Adams Cade, and your expertise."

"Until you pick my brain, then toss the shell of the elite Adams Cade aside." The master inventor, Southern gentleman, family exile and ex-con almost smiled then, as well.

To the rustle of the board's horrified mutterings, Jacob Helms spoke with the thunder of an itinerant evangelist. "Never. That's the beauty of an alliance. Safety."

"So—" Adams folded his hands over his rigid stomach, thumbs tapping a slow tattoo "—what's in it for me besides money?"

"What more would you want?" Jacob Helms and his chorus of yes-men were stymied. "I don't understand."

"No," Adams said softly. "I can see that you don't."

"But would you consider our offer?"

Adams' answer was slow in coming. As he sifted through information garnered over the years on Helms, Helms, and Helms. Which comprised a reputable consortium, taking values to a higher level. An enterprise of honor, guided by men of honor. "Yes."

The response was barely a whisper. In his surprise, Jacob Helms almost dislodged his gold wire rims. "You did say yes?"

Adams nodded. "Yes, sir, I will consider your offer."

Jacob Helms was accustomed to fighting on his own turf. In this, a battle he wasn't sure he would win, he had brought his distinguished board of directors as a show of force. Now the battle seemed to have been won in the first skirmish. Chastising himself for boosting millions to tens of millions, he moved quickly for closure. "Would you shake on that, young man?"

"Would you take the word of an ex-con?" Adams countered.

"I would take the word of Adams Cade no matter that he has been in prison." Bemused, the elderly man reversed, reiterated, "No, I would take the word of Adams Cade *because* he has survived five years in prison and emerged a better man."

"In that case, contingent on the agreement of my staff and certain others..." The telephone at Adams' elbow rang. He almost ignored the insistent summons, but ended in lifting the receiver from its cradle. "Yes, Janet?" A frown pulled at his face, marring the controlled expression. "Jefferson!"

Brown eyes that seemed to lose their touch of silver grew ever more lightless. "Put him through."

The room was quiet, all eyes riveted on Adams Cade, whose heart saw beloved faces present only in yellowing photos. "Jefferson?" Adams neither moved nor spoke again for a long-held breath. Then, softly, he murmured, "Jeffie?"

The childhood name tumbled from a man carrying the

pain and hurt of years. "How are you? Lincoln? Jackson?" In a faltering stumble his voice dropped lower. "How is he? How is...Gus?"

The once pleasant and amiable expression contorted in sorrow. The handsome face turned ashen. As still as death, Adams listened. His body jerked, recoiling from the news. Then he straightened. "I'll be there."

With the receiver halfway to its cradle, he brought it back to his ear. "Jeffie?" Adams hesitated. Then, dreading the answer to the question he must ask, he closed his eyes, shutting his immediate world away. "Did he ask for me?"

Silence swarmed in the room, broken only by the scrape of a shoe. No one moved again. They were strangers, caught in a cruel vacuum until Adams sighed, his chest shuddering. "It's all right," he whispered. "I didn't expect he would.

"Don't! Don't be sorry. No matter what your conscience would have you believe, none of this is your fault." Sighing again roughly, in a voice grown deeper and huskier, he repeated, "I'll still be there, as soon as the plane is ready."

Adams listened again, oblivious of his captive audience. "Not there." His words resounded in irrevocable decision. "I'll come to Belle Terre. Not..." The word *home* hovered on his tongue, then was lost. "Not to the plantation...not to Belle Reve."

The men of Helms listened avidly. Adams didn't care. "From the city limits of Belle Terre to Belle Reve is less than five miles. Hardly a taxing distance.

"Where will I stay?" Adams shook his head, pondering. "I've been away so long I don't know any places. Make some suggestions—I'll have Janet do the rest." Taking up a pen, on a notepad lying squarely in the center of his desk Adams scrawled the sources of lodging in the quaint city. "These should do it. Janet can gather information, then choose for me."

Laying the pen aside, Adams slipped back a cuff to check the time. "Just a matter of hours, Jeffie. Hang tough."

As the receiver rattled into place, Adams Cade stood, only then recalling his visitors. "Gentlemen, I'm afraid we must continue this conference another time. My father is ill. I will be leaving Atlanta immediately."

"You can't go," Jacob Helms snapped with an edge of steel. This was the voice of command, meant to send minions scurrying to do his bidding.

Adams Cade had never been a minion. Anyone in his right mind would doubt he knew how to scurry. "You're mistaken, sir. I can leave. I am leaving."

"We had a deal."

"No, sir," Adams corrected the proper gentleman. "We were on the verge of making a deal with a contingency."

A flush across his cheeks signaled Helms' anger at the upstart's contradiction. As he looked to his board and back again to Adams, he barely managed to quell his ire at being defied, even so genteelly. "We'd spoken our agreement."

"We'd spoken of agreeing to agree, if all elements fell into place. For now, they can't." Adams rested his curled hands on the walnut plane of his pristine work space. "This meeting was your idea, the conditions your choice. Listening to and accepting or not accepting your proposal was mine."

"Was?" Jacob Helms, for all his arrogance, had not built his business empire by being obtuse.

"Yes, sir." Adams straightened. "*Was* is the operative word. Now that choice has been taken from me."

Bracing himself on the desk in a parody of Adams' recent posture, Jacob Helms leaned close. "Your brother calls to say your father is ill, and you're going to delay a multimillion-dollar deal?"

Adams only nodded, not surprised Helms knew he had been discussing his father, and his father's health, with Jefferson.

"For a man who disowned you, a man who will not even look upon your face, you would risk the loss of our offer?"

"For my father I would risk anything. And for my father I must leave." Turning to the board, he spoke pleasantly. "Gentlemen, you must excuse me. I have a plane to catch." With that courtesy and no more heed of Jacob Helms or his multimillion-dollar alliance, he strode from the room.

After an absence that seemed forever, Adams Cade was returning to the South Carolina low country, the land and islands of his youth.

The land, the islands and the father he loved.

One

"He's here, Mrs. Claibourne. And totally dangerous!"

Placing the last blossom in the massive flower arrangement that would soon grace the lanai of the river cottage, Eden Claibourne, mistress of The Inn at River Walk, stepped back. Carefully she inspected her artistry, nodded approval and turned, at last, to address the breathless young woman.

"Where is he, Merrie?" Her voice was hushed, musical, with only a hint remaining of the Carolina low-country accent.

Merrie, the youngest, prettiest and most impressionable of the staff, clasped her hands before her in an effort to calm herself. "I took him to the library as Cullen instructed and assured him you would be there shortly."

"Thank you." A probing look took in the young woman's face, made even prettier by a dark, dancing gaze. Merrie was the daughter of a friend of a friend, a student at the local college and a newcomer to Belle Terre. Yet, obviously, the reputation of the arriving guest had preceded him even into the halls of the inn. "You do realize he isn't dangerous, don't you, Merrie?"

"Not dangerous, Mrs. Claibourne. *Dangerous!* With a capital *D,* because he looks so handsome." Merrie laughed. "That's how the girls in my class would describe him."

"Ah, you're studying slang now?" Eden chuckled, for normally Merrie rarely noticed the opposite sex, handsome or not. The girl's first and last love was horses. "Slang aside, did you offer our guest a drink? Or a glass of chilled wine?"

Merrie's head bobbed, sending an ebony mane ending in curls cascading nearly to her waist. "Mr. Cade prefers wine later, in his room."

"Excellent." A slim hand rested lightly on the girl's shoulder, as Eden Claibourne remembered when Adams Cade had the same effect on her. The vernacular of the time was different, but the effect was definitely the same.

Putting memories best left in the past aside, Eden addressed Merrie in her usual sensible tone. "If you would please ask Cullen to have the wine steward select several wines, then, if he would, take these flowers with the wine to the river cottage, I shall greet our newest guest."

Certain beyond doubt her instructions would be followed to the letter under the critical eye of her head steward, Cullen Pavaouau, Eden Roberts Claibourne hurried to the library.

Through the years many influential guests and many celebrities had chosen to stay in the gracious antebellum home Eden had transformed into an inn. But even before she'd returned to Belle Terre to reclaim and rescue the beautiful old landmark from crumbling ignominy, as

Nicholas Claibourne's wife, she had known what it was to live and move among the wealthy and near wealthy, the famous and soon-to-be famous. Yet in all those times, in all the places the Claibournes' travels had taken them, in all the social and professional circles into which they had been welcomed, no one set excitement ablaze in the heart of the mistress of River Walk as had Adams Cade.

"Good grief! I'm as bad as Merrie." Halting in the cool, broad hall, her hand resting on the carved door that stood slightly ajar and opened into the library, she caught what she intended to be a relaxing breath. Sweeping her pale-brown hair from her face, she adjusted her blouse and brushed a leaf from her slim skirt. Muttering, "Mr. Dangerous with a capital *D,* indeed," Eden squared her shoulders and stepped inside.

He was there. Adams was there, standing with his back to the room, looking out over the grounds and the broadest expanse of the river. Absorbed in his thoughts, he didn't hear her approach, affording her a precious instant to look at him. Time to seek out the changes the years and life and prison had wrought.

He seemed bigger now. Not taller, but more massive. A better fit for the breadth of his shoulders than his youthful slenderness had been. A product of maturity and time. As were, she supposed, the hints of silver threading through his thick, perfectly barbered, perfectly groomed hair.

Eden never knew what disturbance drew him from his thoughts. A raggedly caught breath? Some subtle scrape of her foot over the parquet? The wild-bird flutter of her heart?

As if thirteen years had not passed since he'd seen her, Adams Cade turned, his gaze a solemn touch on her face.

Beneath the elegant, worldly veneer that Eden Claibourne presented, the memories of a young girl quickened and trembled like the unshed tear on the sweep of downcast lashes. Visions of the wild, beautiful young man he'd been danced like living flames in her mind and heart. But when her gaze lifted to his, her eyes were clear, their brightness natural, and she searched the grave and handsome face for some trace of the laughing young rogue.

The rogue she'd loved in her reticent tomboy days. The days when all who knew her called her Robbie and she'd trailed behind Adams and his brothers at every opportunity. Like a shadow attached to his heel, she'd taken every step he took, risked every dare he dared. All for a smile and a teasing ruffle of the riotous curls her grandmother kept cut short.

Now, in the fall of light from the library windows, keeping his gaze, she searched again for the dashing young man the exuberant rogue had become. For Adams, the friend and champion she'd thought lost to her forever in tragedy that sent him to prison. Adams, her first and tender lover.

But in the silvery depths of his magnificent brown eyes, she saw no rogue, no laughter, no memories. Only cool control.

He was the epitome of rugged splendor in his immaculate suit. With the proper shirt, proper tie, proper shoes, the proper haircut, recalling another night he had been splendid, yet not so proper. A night of breathtaking wonder.

Thirteen years had passed since the night of her debut.

She was nineteen then, and a freshman in college. He, twenty-four and, in her eyes, a man of the world. Yet to her delight he agreed to be her escort for the season. Willing, for pesky Robbie Roberts, to suffer the formalities and the endless galas he found annoying and boring. The night of the ball, he was so gallant and so handsome she loved him so much it hurt.

After the presentation and the bows and the ball, as they walked a deserted beach in bare feet and formal clothes and with hands entwined, she never wanted the night to end. When he kissed her in the moonlight, drawing her down to the sand, she went hungrily into his arms. In a struggle for sanity, when he would have drawn away, it was her clumsily worshiping hands that kept him. Her naive touch that seduced.

When sanity was lost, the yards of her white satin gown became their lovers' bower. And in that moment of rapture, the moment when the name he called was Eden, she discovered that the pain of love could be its greatest pleasure.

The night was magic. Adams was magic. And when he kissed her good-night one last time on her doorstep, she never dreamed it would be thirteen years, and this day, before she saw him again.

Thirteen years and a lifetime of remembering.

In a silence that had been only seconds but seemed forever, as she looked into eyes that revealed no secrets, she knew he hadn't forgotten. But she wondered if he ever remembered.

A harsh breath threatened the perfect drape of his jacket as something akin to regret flickered over his face. Yet, with that small lift of his shoulders, he seemed to shake off a mood. Taking a step forward, his hand extended and palm up, he waited with the hard-learned patience of prison.

She wouldn't have refused this silent, cautious man if she'd intended it. She couldn't if she tried. As silently as he, she placed her fingers over his palm and felt the warmth of his firm and gentle clasp.

"Eden."

In a voice barely more than a whisper, he called her name. Not Robbie. Eden. The name he'd said only once before on a moonlit night on the beach. Then she realized her mistake and understood that no matter what terrible things had happened to him, no matter who he had become, Adams Cade had never forgotten, and never stopped remembering.

"Your hair is darker." His voice was low and resonant with the years of added maturity. "I remember blonde curls."

Eden nodded as his gaze ranged over her, from shoulder-length bob to the sweep of her brows and the curve of her cheek. Pausing only the beat of a faltering heart on the tilt of her lips, he let his look glide intimately over the arch of her throat, the soft thrust of her breasts. Then the slender curve of her hips.

"You're taller, more slender," he murmured as the darkness of his gaze retraced its path to meet hers.

"Only a bit," Eden assured him. Though at nearly thirty-two, she knew the softness of youthful curves had gradually become an inadvertent but fashionably angular leanness.

"I never thought to be in Belle Terre again. Nor did I expect to find Robbie Roberts returned as the beautiful, sophisticated Eden Claibourne, innkeeper extraordinaire."

"Nor did I," Eden admitted, regaining a bit of her composure. "But you're here, and I am who I am and what I am. So welcome, Adams, to River Walk, and to my home in Belle Terre." Her fingers still clasped tightly in his, she smiled up at him. "Because I thought you would be tired from your journey, the river cottage is ready and waiting for you."

"Cottage?" He looked down at her in a gaze that was

less guarded, if not yet at ease. "I won't be staying in the inn?"

"Of course you may stay in the house itself, if you wish. But first, take a look." Drawing him back to the window with its view of the grounds and the river, she gestured toward a building. Perched by the river's edge, the single-story structure was nearly hidden by trees and plants scattered about it.

Small, in comparison to the main house, and quaint, it lay in dappled but deepening shadows as the setting sun streamed through moss-draped oaks. Within that shade, immense azaleas, camellias and oleanders blended with palms and palmettos. Clustered so thickly about its courtyard, the groomed and tended plants afforded an additional element of seclusion.

"There are porches on each side, with a lanai and a separate and private walk on the riverside," Eden explained as he studied the cottage with a look of approval. "I thought you might prefer the privacy, at least at first."

Adams nodded, grateful for her thoughtfulness. Returning to the low country, and the harsh days it recalled, was difficult enough without facing curious stares. A day or two of quiet to acclimatize and inure himself in the time and tide of the city would ease the way as much as it could be eased. "Thank you, Eden, for your kindness."

"A consideration more than a kindness, Adams." With a shrug of a shoulder, Eden dismissed the hurried but exacting care that had gone into each detailed preparation for Adams' stay at the inn. Hopefully he would never know the mad furor the knowledge of his impending arrival had inspired.

With belying composure, she paraphrased a lecture she gave the staff almost daily. "Part of the charm of the inn is that we match our services to the unique needs of our guests."

"Then I thank both you and your staff."

Something in his tone made her regret her cavalier dismissal of his gratitude, and especially that she had made him seem to be just another guest. Adams had become a prominent man, a celebrity in the business world. She was sure, for that reason, he had become the object of much catering and courting. No, he wouldn't be a stranger to special attention. But how often from the goodness of an unselfish heart? Because someone cared about Adams himself, rather than the hope of remuneration or favor?

"Adams," she began, and discovered she didn't know how to explain, so she settled for honesty. Touching his cheek as if she would stroke away the pain of lost years and of wounds that had never healed, she spoke from her heart. "I'm glad you've come, and I want you to be comfortable and happy in my home."

Suddenly feeling presumptuous for the liberty she'd taken, Eden drew her hand away and offered her most cheerful smile. "But enough of this." Folding her fingers in her palm, keeping the memory of the feel of his skin beneath her fingertips, she suggested, "You must be tired and hungry after your flight."

"It has been a trying day," Adams admitted as he strove to remember how long it had been since a lovely woman had touched him so gently and smiled only for him.

"Then as meets your pleasure, sir—" Eden inclined her head, in concern and genuine respect for an old friend "—tonight and any other time. You may make of your stay what you wish. Whatever suits your needs—privacy, seclusion, companionship, involvement. Meals in the main dining room or in the cottage. Whatever fits your schedule and your mood will be done to the best of the staff's ability. All you need do is ask, Adams.''

At the moment a quiet meal away from prying eyes and with someone who didn't insist on discussing business incessantly was Adams' pleasure, and the perfect end of a disturbing day. ''Dinner in the cottage sounds wonderful, but I wouldn't want to inconvenience your staff.''

Glad for a chance to put aside the scintillating leap of tension touching him had caused in her, Eden smiled. Then she laughed, recalling how her staff engaged in friendly disputes for the privilege of dodging out of the busy dining room that served citizens of Belle Terre, as well as guests of the inn. Sometimes the break meant a quick smoke. Sometimes simply a breath of fresh air. ''It would never be considered an inconvenience. In fact, there are volunteers anxious to serve you tonight.''

''Then I'd like that, Eden. As I suspect you've already guessed and planned for.'' Turning his back on the view she'd offered, he looked down at her. His gaze touching her hair and her face once again was like a remembered caress. ''I'd like it even better if you would join me.''

His voice was deep and rich, like velvet stroking her skin. Each quiet nuance stirring a longing better left in slumber. ''I usually make a practice of being in the dining room most evenings,'' she demurred. ''Greeting guests, smoothing ruffled feathers when there are any.''

''When there are any,'' he challenged. ''Which is…''

The confident look he gave her made her smile again as she confessed, ''Which—because I have a superb and efficient majordomo, a well-trained and wonderfully loyal staff—is, truthfully, very rarely.''

''Ahh, just as I thought when I arrived. A well-oiled, thoughtfully run operation.'' Tucking her hand in the crook of his arm, he continued to stand before the windows. At his back the sinking sun turned massive oaks dressed in Spanish moss into bewitching shadows etched against the fire of the sky.

"So," he said persuasively, the pad of his thumb stroking her fingers as they curved over the fine fabric of his jacket, "though you would be missed, no guests would cry into his or her vichyssoise or the peaches Grand Marnier, if they must suffer through one night without your lovely smile to greet them?"

At her look of surprise, he chuckled. A slightly wicked sound that triggered more memories and sent her pulse rate into orbit. "You seem to know quite a lot about the inn. Down to our guests' favorite spring specialties."

"Thanks to Janet and no credit to me."

"Janet?" Try as she might, Eden couldn't keep the curious note from her tone. His familiar mention of a woman was startling. For though she couldn't define or explain her conviction, Adams Cade had the look of a man uninvolved and unattached.

"My secretary." His stroking ceased, his hand folded over hers, keeping it against his arm. "My very efficient secretary, who learned quite a lot about The Inn at River Walk, but found no mention of the luxury or the privacy of a river cottage."

"The cottage isn't advertised. We rent it sparingly, keeping it free for guests with special needs."

"Like Adams Cade, the black sheep returned?" Adams grimaced, the touch of wicked teasing faded from his words. "Adams Cade, whose reputation precedes him, I'm sure. At least, if small-town gossips are as I remember."

There was the hurt again. Hurt he thought to hide with brusque conjecture. But neither time nor tragedy had irrevocably changed the timbre of the tones she had learned to read, and loved beyond measure, in days past and months and years.

With the last of laughter flown before pain she would give her soul to heal, Eden met his look solemnly. "Yes," she said, her clasp convulsing over his arm. "For guests like Adams Cade, because he *is* Adams Cade, and very special."

"A convicted felon, an ex-con, a brawler, the disowned black sheep of his family," he said, ticking off only a few of his sins. "How could that make me special?"

"You're none of those things to me," Eden protested. "None. And small-minded gossips with their ugly whispers to the contrary be damned."

Turning to her, taking both her hands in his, Adams searched her face, seeking the bravado, the bluster of a comforting lie. But he found only serene, unshakable honesty. "What was I to you? What am I now, my lovely Eden?"

Eden. The name of a woman, not a favorite tomboy. A name that made her heart sing.

"What were you?" A pensive look touched her eyes and lips as she smiled at him. "So many things."

"Such as?"

"When I was shy and distant, without a clue how to be part of the group, you were my mentor, my champion. You made me feel like a princess, though I was painfully graceless and gawky."

When she hesitated over the next of her memories, Adams spoke into the silence. "You were too pretty and too smart for the rest of us. Never graceless or gawky, except in your own mind."

When he was with her, that was how he made her feel, what he made her believe. From the first, with Adams she was always more and better. Always happier. "When my grandfather brought me with him to Belle Reve…"

"Go on," Adams encouraged. "The name doesn't disturb me. What happened that last night might have taken my home and family from me, but that doesn't mean I've forgotten good times or good memories. I can hear the name and think of Belle Reve and all it stood for without being bitter. So tell me, Eden."

Resisting the urge to clear the pain that lay like a cramp at the base of her throat, Eden was still hesitant. For no matter that he encouraged her, she had to believe that speaking of the family and the home he'd been denied would open old wounds.

"When your grandfather brought you…" he prompted, and smiled through hidden sadness when her gray gaze probed his.

"When my grandfather brought me with him to Belle Reve to treat the horses—" Eden, defeated, took up the thread of her story "—I was enchanted by the house, the land and what seemed like herds and herds of horses. But most of all I was enchanted by you.

"Even if you deny it, Adams Cade, I was graceless, I was gawky, I stuck with you like a cocklebur. Yet you were patient and kind beyond belief. You were older, but you never treated me like a nuisance." Smiling into his steady gaze, Eden murmured, "When I look back, I count you as my first and best friend."

"And now, Eden?" There was raw need in his look. A strong man's need for a friend.

Eden wanted to end the hurt, silence the rejection. She wished that by caring, she could free him from the control that ruled his life. Replace this cautious, solemn stranger with the wonderfully wicked charmer of old. She wanted to hold him, comfort him. And if he should love her…

Abandoning a thought that was going where she never intended, a thought she dared not pursue, she kept his gaze. "You were my friend. I hope you will be again."

Perhaps if he would be, this time she could repay the kindnesses that were most instrumental in molding her into the confident woman she'd become.

All of Belle Terre knew the irascible Gus Cade had fallen ill. All knew of the dissension in the Cade family. In the years since Adams was convicted of aggravated assault, Gus had made no secret of his bitter resentment of the disgrace his oldest son had brought to the family name. An opinion some of Belle Terre would share. One others, even most, would not. While Adams stayed at River Walk, she would be his champion as he had been hers. And God help any who uttered a harsh judgment within her hearing.

"I'm to be your friend and you will be mine, right?" Adams looked down at her, the edge of tension easing from his face. With her hands still nestled in his, the pads of his thumbs traced lazy caresses over her knuckles. "Then you can begin by having dinner with me at the cottage."

"You said you were tired," Eden protested. "And surely you will want to speak with your brothers."

"If I'm tired, you're the most restful thing that's happened to me in a long while. I spoke to my brothers from the airport shortly after landing. If there's any change in Gus' condition, Lincoln and Jackson and Jefferson all know I'm here. None of them would hesitate to call. And I'm sure your efficient staff would see to it the call was put through to me.

"So as it stands now, all bases are covered. In the meantime, Eden, my sweet, I'm holding you to your promise."

"My promise?" Eden had made no promises she remembered.

"'Then as meets your pleasure, tonight and any other time, you may have whatever you wish,'" he quoted word for word.

"Oh." Eden blushed at the implication of the words.

"Yes, 'oh.' And my pleasure tonight would be a quiet dinner in the cottage, in your company." His low laughter teased, almost as in the past. "Give it up, sweetheart. I have you cornered. You're caught on your own hook. You promised, and something tells me you're a woman who keeps promises."

"This is blackmail," Eden accused. Demurring, even as she knew that when he was like this—so much like the boy and the young man she'd known and loved—she could deny him nothing.

"Perhaps it is, but you won't refuse."

Eden saw then that the old confidence was there. With it, the added confidence of a survivor. The confidence of brilliance that could analyze a problem, then create a solution that would bring him to the forefront of the business world. Confidence that had faltered only in the land of Belle Terre and Belle Reve, where his father lay grievously ill.

Confidence that lived and would continue to live within the walls and grounds of River Walk. Eden was adamant.

"No," she admitted after a thoughtful pause, "I won't refuse. I will have dinner with you in the cottage."

But not like this. She would not go to the man she had loved all her life grubby from a day's work. "Why don't we both freshen up? Merrie, the young woman you met earlier, will show you to the cottage and take your order for dinner."

"I would prefer that you choose. My tastes haven't changed so much."

"All right, I'll see to that first, then come to the cottage in forty-five minutes or so. That should give you time to settle in, have a drink and relax a bit before dinner."

"You will come to the cottage?" he asked in a tone she couldn't fathom. "Your word on it, Eden?"

"My most solemn word, Adams."

"Then I'll wait here for Merrie." Satisfied at last, releasing her, he stepped away and, with a gallant bow, settled in a chair by the window.

He was still sitting there lost in his thoughts when Eden passed by on her return from the kitchen. Pausing, her hand on a curved stair rail, she watched through the open library door and remembered. "Adams, in my home," she murmured, then she smiled as she climbed the stairs to her third-floor apartment.

"Have you wondered what simple soul gave such a beautiful body of water the unimaginative name of Broad River?" Eden leaned against a column as the last of day faded from river and sky. The dinner she'd shared with Adams was long finished, Cullen's carefully supervised choice of wines nearly gone.

"It is magnificent," Adams agreed. "Evenings like this are among the things I miss most."

"The quiet time. Watching the play of color over the water. First the blues, which deepen to turquoise, then navy. Next comes the fire, wild and glittering. Then gradually the darkness seeps in, and reds become burgundy and maroon. Then simply black." Eden spoke as if with her voice she might break the peaceful spell that had fallen over the evening.

"All the better to reflect the silver path of the moon."

The equally subdued, masculine voice drifted out of the darkness.

Adams sat in the recesses of the lanai, hidden within gathering dusk. But with the creak of the swing and the pad of his footsteps, Eden knew he'd come to join her at the railing. Once upon a time he'd smelled of sunlight, sea air and soap. Now, when he was near, she thought of boardrooms, shuffling papers and expensive cologne. But that could change.

"You could come back, Adams." He was near, so near she could touch him if she dared. "You could come home again. If not to the plantation, then to Belle Terre."

Adams only shook his head. He didn't want to speak of the past or even the future. He didn't want to think of anything but Eden. Trailing the tip of a finger up the back of her arm, letting the flowing georgette of her long, full sleeve add its own caress to his, he moved a step closer. "Thank you for this—the welcome, the cottage, dinner and the wine. And especially for the company." He laughed softly. "Even the floor show."

"We aim to please." Eden chuckled huskily in response. Even while she fought to quell a shiver as his touch sent a fever shimmering over her skin in the blazing wake of his body heat. She knew his touch was not hot, yet it burned into her, deliciously seducing her. Mindlessly, hardly aware that she spoke, she murmured, "Mother Nature gets credit for the floor show."

"She's quite a beautiful lady. And so are you."

Looking away from the river, she found Adams looming over her. A tall, dark form with the touch of heated velvet and a voice as smooth. "I'm not really beautiful, Adams. Perhaps it's a trick of the light, the rosy glow. Or a mood or the wine. I'm only Eden, and once just Robbie, one of the guys."

"You are beautiful. It isn't a trick, a glow, the moon, or the wine. And, sweetheart—" his drawl was unconsciously seductive "—it's been a long time since you were one of the guys."

At her look of surprise, Adams' first instinct was to fold her in his arms, to show her in ways words never could that she was beautiful. So beautiful the memory of her moonlit image had been strength and solace for a lonely man in the worst days of prison.

He'd dreamed of touching her then. He wanted to touch her now as a lover, as he had only once before. But that was a lifetime ago. Too much had happened. The Adams Cade she'd made love with on a sandy beach was not the man with her now.

He'd lived too long among the hardened and the ruthless. To survive he acquired their brutal ways and habits, the ways and habits of power. He lived his life as best he could, with honor and in truth. But deep inside he'd grown hard and bold, taking what he wanted, keeping it for only as long as he wanted.

He'd known beautiful women. But never in love. Never in tenderness. And no matter how he searched, none had been Eden.

Now she was here, only a forbidden touch away. The same sweet Eden, unsullied beneath the worldly elegance. But in the harshness that marked his life, he was wrong for her.

Perhaps they could be friends, as she asked. But never lovers, as he wished.

"It's late," he declared firmly, the rush of his breath warming her cheek. "This has been a long day for both of us."

Catching the scarf draped like a shawl about her shoulders, he drew her close. Touching his lips to her forehead, he savored the feel and fragrance of her. But knowing this was all he could have of her, all that he dared, he put her from him.

Stroking her cheek with the back of his hand, he whispered, "You're tired. I've asked too much of you this day."

"No—"

A finger brushing her lips silenced her protest. "Come," he insisted, taking her hand. "I'll walk you home."

She didn't protest again. Not even when he kissed the sensitive flesh of her wrist, thanking her most gallantly for a lovely evening and for the pleasure of her company. Nor when he left her in the shadow of the sprawling back porch of River Walk.

Eden watched until the darkness washed over him and hid him from sight. She watched and waited, but he didn't turn, he didn't look back. And he didn't hear as she whispered. "Good night, Adams Cade."

Then, in a voice husky with tears, as Cullen stepped from the shadows, she whispered, "Good night, Adams, my love."

Two

"**M**rs. Claibourne."

Eden looked up from the basket of flowers she was gathering while they were still glittering with dew. Shading her eyes against the early-morning sun, she realized that it was Merrie rushing toward her. As the girl came closer, Eden saw her face was flushed, her eyes bright, and the lovely mass of dark curls tumbled in fey disorder down her back.

Certain something was dreadfully wrong, Eden slipped off the supple leather gloves she used for gardening. Tucking gloves and shears into a pocket, she waited for the outburst.

Standing in the rising heat of the unseasonably warm spring morning, she watched Merrie weaving though the garden and wondered what problem had thrown this most vivacious member of her staff into a dither. Visions of termites swarming over the lower porches or mice in the pantry filled her thoughts, even as she knew that termites and mice would never cause this agitation in one so new to the foibles of ancient Southern homes.

"There's more!" Merrie stopped, barely avoiding Eden.

"Whoa!" Eden exclaimed as she steadied the girl. "Calm down and tell me what in heaven's name has you so excited. There's more, you say? More of what?"

"More of them," Merrie managed between heaving gasps.

"'Them'?" Eden lifted a questioning brow as she found the oblique answer even more puzzling. "What? Who?"

"The other presidents."

Eden was totally baffled now. "What presidents? Where?"

"The Cades." Merrie caught a long breath, then spoke more calmly in faultless English just acquiring a touch of the Southern lilt. "In the library. The inn is full of them. The more they come, the more dangerous they are. Except for the first."

"Adams' brothers," Eden interpreted rather than asked, not really certain having the three younger, brawling Cades on the premises was less disconcerting than termites on the porch or mice in the pantry. Disconcerting or not, it would be interesting, she thought as she continued her interpretation. "And, as with Adams, dangerous meaning handsome—or better."

"Mr. Adams' brothers," Merrie confirmed. "But totally different and totally handsome."

"And these presidents are in the library?" Eden chuckled in spite of knowing she really shouldn't encourage such unbridled exuberance in her staff. Still, she doubted Merrie's initial reaction would last. Not even a bevy of dangerously handsome men could supersede her greatest love.

"Since that was where you asked me to take Mr. Adams when he arrived, I was sure it would serve for the rest of the family."

"Of course it does," Eden agreed. "You did well. But next time, try to announce them with a little more composure."

"I'm sorry." Merrie was instantly contrite. "It's just that no one warned me that the men of Southern North America were so...so..." Shrugging away her loss of words, she settled simply for redundancy. "Dangerous."

Eden wondered if she should explain that the Cades were a breed apart, and certainly not men against whom others could be measured. But, deciding some things were better learned than told, she kept silent, waiting for Merrie to complete her report.

"They asked to see Mr. Adams," the girl continued as expected. "Since you gave strict orders that he was to have no unannounced visitors unless you screened them, I thought the library was best. Mrs. Claibourne, I hope it was all right that I asked Cullen to see if they wanted coffee and muffins."

"That's perfect, Merrie. What you did was exactly right."

"Should I get Mr. Adams now? Or take the gentlemen down to the river cottage?"

"No," Eden said thoughtfully. "I think not just yet." Given Merrie's description, she didn't doubt that it was Adams' brothers who waited in the library. She couldn't think of a soul who would be brave enough, or foolhardy enough, to misrepresent themselves as Cades. Even so, she would see for herself and judge the mood of this visit before Adams was disturbed.

"These flowers are for the suite in the west wing," she told Merrie with her usual calm. "The Rhetts are scheduled to arrive just after lunch. In case I'm delayed with the Cades, would you see to arranging them and getting them to the suite?" Anticipating the answer, Eden offered the dew-laden flowers.

"Of course." Merrie took the basket. "My mother often asked me to do the flowers when she entertained."

"I know. Do your best, Merrie. That's all I ask."

"I will, Mrs. Claibourne."

"I know," Eden said again. She'd spoken truthfully. She did know Merrie would do an excellent job. All the staff at the inn put their best effort into any task they were assigned. Eden had striven to assure their working conditions were pleasant and rewarding. In turn the staff was phenomenally efficient. So efficient that Eden was confident that even in her absence, the inn would continue as usual.

Grateful for her good fortune and anticipating a meeting with old friends, she hurried to the house. Even as the back hall door closed behind her, Eden heard their voices. Deep, masculine voices. Familiar voices she had known all her life.

The library door was ajar and her step was quiet, but not one of the stunning and uniquely different young men was unaware of her entrance. In an instant each was on his feet, vying to be first to hug her, first to kiss her. And in Jackson's case, she feared, first to threaten the strength of her ribs.

It would have been overwhelming if the anticipated jousting hadn't been a common occurrence since she'd known them. They were the Cades, not just a breed apart from other men, but among themselves. Yet, in their differences, once they had been a close family. Eden hoped they could be again.

"Lincoln," she said in greeting as the tallest, and second oldest, took command, virtually lifting her off her feet.

Before his kiss was finished, she was snatched away by Jackson, the fiery one. Whose exuberant bear hug, as expected, literally took her breath away.

"Hey, brother, don't break her in half or you'll have our older brother to contend with," Jefferson said as he gently extricated her from Jackson's brawny arms.

Jefferson, the quietest of the four, clasped her shoulders, looking her up and down as if inspecting her for injuries. Then he laughed, muttered something about being indestructible and beautiful, and drew her in his arms. "How are you, Robbie?" he murmured against her cheek. Then, in a breath, "How is he?"

Putting her from him, but not letting go of her hand, he asked in an oddly desperate tone, "How is Adams?"

"He was tired when he arrived, and deeply concerned about Gus. But one of the staff informed me he had an early breakfast. Though not so early that I would think he didn't sleep well. I'm hoping that means he's rested." Going with Jefferson to the sofa, she took the seat he offered.

For all that he lacked in compassion, Gus Cade had never stinted on social instructions for his sons. They might have been prone to mischief and each had scattered the wildest of oats, but few in conventional and proper Belle Terre could match Jefferson, Jackson or Lincoln for gallantry. And only one could best them, Eden recalled. Only the first of them. Only Adams.

Taking the coffee Lincoln poured from a silver server and cream from the pitcher Jackson offered, she sipped dutifully before continuing her report. "Adams is staying in the river cottage. I thought it would be more suitable for your reunion."

Eden knew that in direct defiance of Gus Cade's decree, the brothers had seen each other sporadically over the years. But never in Belle Terre. Never so close to home and Gus.

None of them wanted to hurt Gus, but nor were they willing to abandon their brother as the father had. Secrecy and distance had been the answer. Yet when Adams came to River Walk, Eden hadn't doubted that Lincoln, Jackson and Jefferson would come, as well.

Looking from one startlingly attractive, startlingly different brother to the next, Eden wondered why life had become so busy that they saw each other so little. Even so, she knew she mustn't keep them. None would think of rushing her, but she realized that beneath the decorum they were eager to be with Adams.

"When I went to the garden this morning, the grounds-keeper said he had seen Adams down by the river-cottage dock. I assume he's still there."

"He's here," Adams' voice drifted to them from the open doorway. "Dropping off some fish for dinner."

Clasping her cup tightly to keep from dropping it, Eden looked to the door. Before his brothers surrounded him, she saw the perfectly barbered hair was disheveled, the perfectly tailored suit had been exchanged for a cotton shirt and denims, the perfectly shined shoes for sneakers. Best of all, in the smile he flashed at her, she saw the ghost of the young man she'd loved.

Lincoln was first to speak as they clasped hands to fore-arms as they had as boys. "I've waited for this, for the day you would come home."

"Not home, Linc, but close enough, I suppose."

Though his pleasure in being with his brothers was heartfelt, the hurt in Adams' eyes was not so skillfully hidden. "But wherever, whenever, it's good to see you. All of you."

."Adams." Jackson clasped the other arm. Each man's brawny forearm was aligned, with their hands circling the muscles barely below the elbow of the other. A salute began as a secret ritual of boys survived to become the affectionate gesture of men.

Watching discreetly, Eden wondered how many times she had seen these proud, vigorous men display their affection. That the brothers loved one another and their father deeply was forever evident. Only Gus, who had driven his sons without mercy, judged without compassion, had never offered an iota of affection.

Only Jefferson, the youngest, had ever seemed to matter to the caustic old man. Being Gus' favorite might have made Jefferson's life easier in some ways. But, as few could understand, Eden knew that in the ways that mattered most it made his life far more difficult.

Perhaps there was some explanation for the special bond that had always existed between Adams, the whipping boy, and Jefferson, the favored son. One even Eden could never fathom. It was simply a tie none but the Cades could understand.

As Lincoln and Jackson stepped away from Adams, Jefferson was there, standing before him. Not touching him, not speaking, only looking. No two men could look less like brothers. But with a single glance, any but a fool would know.

In spite of the fact that one was dark-haired and dark-eyed, while the other was blond with blue eyes, there were inexplicable similarities. Similarities caught in a look, a gesture, a tilt of the head. The flash of a smile. A rare laugh.

They were all sons of Caesar Augustus Cade, but with different mothers. Not one bore any resemblance to Gus, except in pride and determination. In looks, each was his mother's son.

In choosing his wives, Gus had seemed determined to create a family as diverse as possible. Adams' mother was of French descent. Lincoln's, a Scot. Jackson's was Irish. And Jefferson's, a Dane. All women with nothing in common except uncommon beauty and a distinct lack of staying power. Thus, with nothing of Gus, the common denominator, in their physical makeup there was little reason for the existence of any other similarities. Yet, with their strong-willed father the only constant force in their young lives, there existed an indefinable element proving they were brothers, and men of a kind.

Eden couldn't explain the phenomenon in the past. She couldn't explain it now. But as Adams and Jefferson faced each other in a room gone silent, she was never more aware of it.

Beyond the windows the garden was alive with birdsong. In the freshening breeze live oaks swayed and whispered, the old house shifted and creaked. Every sound seemed magnified, and every observer frozen in place as the odd moment dragged by.

Then Adams smiled and hooked a palm around the younger man's neck to draw him into a brother's rough embrace. "Jeffie."

The childhood name eased the building tension. Soon all four were laughing, talking at once. Setting down her cup, meaning to slip away, Eden circled around them to the door. She'd almost reached her goal when an arm slid around her waist. Gentle fingers splayed circumspectly over her midriff drew her back against a hard, brawny chest.

Adams. She would know his touch anywhere, anytime.

"Where do you think you're going?" He leaned so close his breath fanned a stray tendril that curled against her throat. "You aren't escaping us so easily."

Laughing, with a sense of old times revisited, Eden turned, expecting he would release her. Instead, she found herself standing in the circle of his arms as he kept her close.

"I wasn't escaping, Adams." She was pleased she could speak naturally when he touched her with familiar intimacy.

"Then you always sidle out the door like a shadow?" Adams lips tilted in the smallest of smiles. "Strange. Of all the things I remember about you, that isn't one of them."

Eden cast a startled look at Adams, but saw no hint of double entendre. "I wasn't sidling. I wasn't escaping." Still caught in his embrace, she drew herself up to her proudest posture. She had grown taller through the years, but Adams was still taller. "I wanted to give you privacy with your family."

By the suddenly solemn look that gave a hard edge to his features, she knew he realized she'd caught the fleeting moment of tension with Jefferson. In the same look she saw that an explanation would be a long time coming. If ever.

Secrets. There were secrets where once there had been only open trust. Perhaps it was another manifestation of the changes prison had wrought? The wedge a hard and alien life could drive into the heart of a family? Yet why with only Jefferson and not with Lincoln and Jackson?

It made no sense. But Eden knew it had been all too real.

"Stay, Eden," Adams insisted. "My brothers and I will have plenty of time later for private talks. Being together as we are is like old times. I know better than anyone that what's been done can't be undone, and I know the choices of youth have changed all of us. For now, let's not think of choices and what can't be changed. Instead, let's remember the way things were."

"Hear! Hear!" Lincoln said quietly, but with his piercing gray gaze meeting his brother's curiously.

"Yes," Jackson joined in. Catching the spirit of Adams' wishes, he snatched up his half-filled coffee cup. Holding it aloft as if it were a flute of champagne, with a slanted grin, he proposed a toast. "To the way things were."

For a startled instant, no one moved. Then, one by one, with Eden leading the way, Adams and Lincoln and Jefferson each took up his own cup. Over a rumble of chuckles and the clatter of converging cups, Adams recalled another tradition from their past. "One Cade for all, and all Cades for one."

In a continuation of that single move, he turned to Eden, his gaze touching hers, keeping it, and he added as he always had in the last of those youthful years, "And for Robbie."

"For Robbie," the younger Cades exclaimed, turning in concert, bowing with a natural gallantry rivaling that of their fictional heroes, Alexandre Dumas' musketeers.

Adams called her Robbie now, and it seemed only fitting for the mood and the time it recalled. Eden hadn't forgotten the hours she'd spent lying on sandy dunes basking in the sun, while Adams read the wonderful adventures aloud. No matter how many times they heard the stories, neither she nor the Cades ever seemed to tire of them. For her, the fascination was the beauty and the pageantry, and Adams' voice. For the brothers, she always felt it was the camaraderie, the honor and the loyalty. And, perhaps, a gentle dream that offered shelter from a stringent, demanding life and the volatile wrath of their father.

She accepted their homage with learned grace. As she accepted, a look at Jefferson had her wondering almost sadly if changes wrought by choices and by deeds that could never be undone would make recapturing that innocent loyalty impossible.

"To Eden."

Adams' voice drew her from thoughts bordering on morose. Thoughts she mustn't let color his homecoming. Looking up from her mesmerized study of the dark liquid in her cup, she found herself held in the snare of his fascinating eyes.

"Once our Robbie," he said, lifting the cup higher. "Now the beautiful and exquisite Eden Claibourne."

"To Eden," the Cades called out in unison, with smiles alight and cups held high.

A twinkle in Jackson's glance made her fearful for the safety of her cups. But instead of sending the delicate china crashing into the fireplace, he returned his to the silver tray. "Enough," he declared with a wink at Eden. "If I drink any more of the River Walk brew, I won't sleep for a week."

"Since you met Inga the indefatigable, you haven't slept in a week, anyway."

Lincoln's droll remark drew a spate of laughter and a comment from Jefferson. "By the way, Lincoln, what happened to sleepless in Belle Terre? With Alice, was it?"

With that bit of nonsense, the familiar wrangling began.

For Eden it was truly like stepping into the past. A glance at Adams made her realize that even though he knew too little of his brothers' lives now, he was nevertheless enjoying the banter.

For this short time memories of his exile and his father's threatened health could be put aside. But all too soon, as she knew it must, the teasing lost its verve, and one by one the younger Cades fell as silent as their brother.

Leaving her place on the sofa, Eden wandered away, intent on setting herself apart as she sensed a time of serious discussion. Discussions in which even Robbie would be an intruder. She'd taken a seat at the window when the quiet ended.

It was Adams who brought to a close the thoughtful pause that threatened to stretch into an uncomfortable silence. "I called the hospital this morning."

"Then you know." Jefferson looked up from his intent study of the intricate patterns of the aged Persian carpet.

"That Gus will be released tomorrow with a team of nurses to care for him?" Adams nodded and raked a hand across the back of his neck as if he would rub away the tension. "Yes, I know." Bleakly, he met his brother's waiting gaze. "It was disturbing to be required to prove I have the right to ask.

"My first thought was that Gus knew I was coming, and it was by his decree that I would be denied information. Then I realized that none of the names of the staff were familiar. Doc Wilson has retired?"

"Three years ago," Jackson supplied with regret in his tone. "One of us should have remembered to tell you."

"In the scope of all that's happened, it doesn't matter." Adams shrugged aside the oversight. He knew that in the thirteen years he'd been away, there would have been many changes he couldn't know about. "From what the doctor told me, Gus really isn't much improved, and there's nothing more the hospital can do for him that the nurses can't do at…at Belle Reve."

Eden saw in his brothers' faces that each recognized Adams' reluctance to call Belle Reve home. The sorrow she saw spoke of the memory that it was the eldest of Gus Cade's sons who loved their father and their home the most.

Adams, Gus' whipping boy. The devoted son who bore his father's wrath without comment or rancor. The gentleman brawler, who laughed his way through countless battles and never held a grudge. Adams, the unexpected and tender lover who, on the night of her debut, had risen from their sandy bower to ride into Rabb Town, the isolated settlement of the Rabbs, the Cades' most bitter rivals. The beloved brother and friend who had inexplicably beaten Junior Rabb within an inch of his life, then silently endured five years in prison, the eternal damnation of his father and exile from his family.

An act without recent provocation and far too costly. None of it made sense, and Adams had never offered any explanation, never claimed any defense. Instead, for a night of strange retribution, he had lost all he loved and all that mattered in his young life.

"I couldn't believe it then," Eden murmured on a low sigh. "I can't believe it now." Clasping her hands in her lap, she shook her head vehemently. "I won't believe it. Ever."

"Talking to yourself, sweet Eden?" Lincoln stood over her, a quizzical look on his handsome face. "Do we bore you that much with our reminiscing?"

Mustering a smile, Eden assured him he was mistaken. "You don't bore me. A woman would have to be dead to be bored with the illustrious Cades. Especially with all four in the same room.''

''Illustrious, huh?'' Lincoln sat down beside her and took her hand in his. ''That's what you were muttering about?''

''Maybe.''

''Or maybe you were remembering the Adams who carried your heart in his hands?'' At her sharp look, he smiled kindly. ''You thought no one noticed? That, as young as we were, we couldn't see? Sweetheart, all of us knew, even Jefferson at just thirteen. All except Adams, that is…until it was too late.''

''Why did he go there, Lincoln? Why to Rabb Town?'' Eden asked the question she'd asked herself a thousand times. A question that never seemed to have an answer. ''Why would he ride horseback all those miles through dangerous swamps and rough trails? Adams harbored no ill will for the Rabbs. They were the ones, they bore the animosity, hating everyone. Junior most of all. I don't understand. None of it made any sense thirteen years ago. It makes no sense now.''

''I know, Eden.'' Lincoln shrugged, but Eden knew it wasn't in dismissal of her concern or for lack of caring.

''What do you think, Lincoln?'' He was an intuitive man, a veterinarian of uncanny talents, as her grandfather had been. Since her return to Belle Terre, Eden had heard the locals discuss his unique diagnostic skills. Among those who raised horses, it was a favorite topic over dinner at River Walk. Eden couldn't believe Lincoln's insight was restricted to the animals he treated. ''Tell me,'' she pleaded. ''Surely you must have some theory, some thoughts on what happened that night.''

Lincoln sat beside her. His hands gripping his knees, his head down, he was caught up in thoughts her questions raised. "What do I think?" he asked at last. "Or what do I know?"

Eden's heart leaped at the idea there might be some evidence in Adams' favor. Before the thought was completed, she knew its folly. If Lincoln knew anything to debunk the Rabbs' claims, anything to disprove the sheriff's case, he would have spoken up long ago. Even so, she wanted to hear what this wisest of Adams' brothers might say. "Tell me. Please."

"It isn't much, sweet Eden." Lincoln's large, work-worn hand covered hers as it rested against her thigh. "It's all conjecture at best and because I know my brother."

"I don't care about the whys or wherefores, Lincoln," Eden exclaimed in a low, ragged voice. "I only want to know what you think and what you believe." Her voice dropped to a whisper he could barely hear. "I don't need to know why or how you came to believe it."

"Shh," Lincoln quieted her with a gentle squeeze of her hand. "Shh." With his calm reaching out to her, he waited until the quick catch in her breath slowed and the flush faded from her cheeks. In all the time since she'd returned to Belle Terre, in the too-rare times their paths had crossed, he'd never seen the coolly sophisticated Eden Claibourne so wonderfully alive.

More than that, he'd never seen a woman so much in love. His brother's life had been hard and tragic. But no man had ever been as fortunate as Adams was in Eden.

"What I believe is that my brother is innocent." As eyes a shade darker than his own held his look steadily, a wry, humorless smile rippled across his craggy face. "What I think is that he's hiding something. Perhaps to protect someone."

"To protect..." Eden began, then faltered. "But who? Why? What person or persons would command such loyalty and love that he would sacrifice his own life to keep them safe?''

''I've asked myself that question more times than I can count. The answer is always the same. I don't know. The night of your debut was a rare night when all of us were home, except Adams. Gus and Jackson and I were up the whole night helping a mare through a difficult foaling. Jefferson was asleep in his bed. You were home before one.'' Lifting a shoulder, he murmured, ''All the people he loved enough to sacrifice himself for, safe and sound and accounted for. Who does that leave? I've racked my brains about it for years, and the answer is always no one.''

''Yet you think this is the explanation.''

''Can you think of another?''

Eden looked at Adams, deep in conversation with the youngest of his brothers. ''No,'' she said softly. ''None at all.''

Lincoln's theory made sense of a nonsensical situation. It explained why a man would offer no defense for a near fatal attack he was too levelheaded to have truly committed. But it was a theory that brought her back to the ever-unanswered question.

''Who?''

A tall, dark figure loomed in the doorway, massive shoulders filling the allotted space. An immaculately tailored khaki uniform matched the equally immaculate Stetson clasped in a strong hand. Yet another gray gaze of yet another degree of darkness perused the room, studying each person, absorbing every nuance and every detail, before pausing at last on Adams.

As if he had been waiting for this moment, Adams looked up, one powerful gaze clashing with another.

"Hello, Jericho, I've been wondering when you would be along."

"Adams." Jericho Rivers nodded, and the star pinned on his chest gleamed dully in the light. Turning to each of the other occupants of the room, he nodded greetings. "Jackson. Jefferson. Lincoln." The deep voice softened. "Eden. I hope you don't mind that I insisted Cullen show me in."

"Of course not. Come in, Jericho." Rising, Eden went to meet him. "Is there something I can do for you?"

"Thank you, no, Eden." The hand she'd shaken returned to the Stetson, turning it again in slow, lazy circles. "I just dropped by for a chat with Adams."

"You going to run me out of Dodge, Sheriff?"

"Nothing so drastic." Something almost like a smile glinted in the marvelous gray eyes of the sheriff. "Just thought you should be told Junior Rabb knows you're here. Junior carries a grudge forever. I'd watch my back, if I were you."

"Thanks, Jericho, I will."

"Good," the sheriff said softly. "And when you get a chance, if you'd stop by the office, I have some questions."

"The case was closed long before you took office, Jericho," Adams reminded him.

"I know," Jericho said mildly. "But humor me in this."

"If you insist. I don't have any answers, Sheriff," Adams said pleasantly. "But you can ask."

"I will," Jericho assured him, even more pleasantly. Then with a last gallant nod for Eden, he was gone, swallowed by the shadows in the hall. But leaving all eyes of those in the library turned curiously toward Adams.

Three

"Good morning."

Eden looked up from the sheaf of papers scattered over her breakfast table and found herself face-to-face with a man who looked more like a grizzly than a guest who would wish anyone a good anything. More like a grizzly with festering thorns in his paws to be exact.

"Good morning, Adams," she replied cheerfully, as if his greeting had been pleasant. "This is quite a surprise. I didn't expect to see you here."

"No? Is there some reason I shouldn't be here?" His normally handsome brows wrinkled and lowered over dark, silvered eyes. His stormy gaze shifted from her. Piercing and steely, his scrutiny raked over the wait staff beginning preparations for the noon rush, clashed briefly with Cullen's stolid regard, then moved on, unconcerned by the warning he saw there.

Next to catch his attention was the eclectic mix of

guests tarrying to gossip over morning coffee. All of whom, Eden noted unhappily, were more attuned to the charming sunlit luxury of the River Walk dining room than he was.

"You're my guest, Adams. There would never be any reason you aren't welcome here," she assured him with forced cheer as she ignored his glowering mood. "I was simply making conversation. In innkeeper's language, my next comment would have been, 'I hoped you slept well.'"

A commiserating shake of her head and a graceful lift of her shoulders accompanied a meaningful pause. "But judging from evidence to the contrary and an attitude suggesting you've come looking for a fight, I suppose I must presume your night was less than restful."

"Then you would presume wrong," he snarled with no improvement in attitude. "The night was fine. I slept fine. I'm fine. I didn't come here looking for a fight."

"Oh?" Eden muttered half under her breath. "You could have fooled me."

This time Adams ignored her. "What I came looking for was a change of scenery."

"Well then, the inn and its grounds can certainly offer that." Calling on years of experience in smoothing the ruffled feathers of temperamental guests, Eden suggested placidly, "If that isn't enough, the staff and I will do whatever we can to make your surroundings and your stay more pleasant. If we've left something undone, Adams, we'll correct it. If you have some special need, we'll try to meet it."

"Save the spiel, Madam Innkeeper," he groused. "You know damned well there's nothing wrong with the service. Or the grounds, or the view, the cottage, my bed, or anything."

When Adams had ticked each off irritably, he stopped abruptly, his teeth clenched. A muscle rippled in his jaw, a rasping breath lifted his chest and strained the knit of his shirt. Then, as if that breath were a panacea, or perhaps had stirred the voice of reason, a rueful smile quirked the corner of his mouth as he ducked his head in mild disgust. "Ah hell, Eden, the truth is, I'm sick to death of my own company."

Leaning back in her chair, Eden folded her hands in her lap. "So you came looking for different company."

"No." Adams' denial was decisive, abrupt.

"No?"

"No!" In another flash of angry unrest, he lashed out. "Dammit, Eden, is there an echo in here?"

"I don't think so, Adams." Her low tone was mild, almost musical, and soothing. "At least I never heard it before today."

"Enough!" Reaching over the small table to curl his fingers around the beveled edges of the arms of Eden's chair, he braced his hands on either side of her. Leaning close, speaking deliberately, in carefully enunciated syllables, Adams spelled out his seething frustration. "I didn't come looking for company, and I didn't come to discuss how I did, or didn't, sleep. Or damnable echoes. I came for you, for Eden Claibourne."

"Why?" He was so close the expensive and too-proper scent that recalled boardrooms and mountains of paper assailed her. Her heart was racing. If she hadn't clasped them tightly in her lap, her hands would have been shaking. Yet her gaze remained cool and unwavering, revealing nothing.

"Why?" he parroted. *"Why?"* This last he accompanied with a long, heated glare.

"Yes, Adams. Why?"

Throwing up his hands, he muttered, "Ah, hell, there goes that blasted echo again."

Eden laughed, and was pleased at the natural sound of it. "I'm sorry. We do sound like echoes, don't we?" Leaning forward, fingers laced and steady, she asked, "Now, what can I do for you this lovely morning?"

Unappeased by her apology, he bolted from the table and paced away. But only a little way before he turned back, his gaze riveted on her. "What you can do for me is stop avoiding me."

"But I'm not. I haven't." The second the denials were spoken, Eden knew they were a lie. A lie she couldn't let stand.

Trading the death grip of her clasped hands for the stability of the table, she rested her hands on the creamy linen tablecloth. Only a little less than candidly, she admitted her sin. "Okay, it's true, I have been avoiding you. But only because I know this is a difficult situation for you and I felt you needed space and some time alone."

"I don't need space. I don't need time. And I certainly don't need to be alone. God knows, I've had more than enough of all three in the last week. More than I can stand, believe me." He could have spoken of the loneliness of five years in prison. The gut-wrenching sickness of being lost and alone, even among the crowd of inmates. He could have said many things, but he didn't. Adams had never spoken of that black hole of despair and torment to anyone. He didn't think he ever could.

Raking his hand through his wealth of brown hair, thoroughly disturbing its usual order before his fingers curled into impotent fists, he strove again for a smile. An effort that fell short. "What I need now is a friend."

Wearily, Adams Cade, dynamic entrepreneur, hardened alumnus of a brutal prison system, made an admission he never thought he would. "Dammit, I need you, Eden. I need to remember there's still gentleness and grace in the world."

"And you want this gentleness and grace from me?" Her mouth was dry, and her low tone had grown husky and unsteady, but in his agitation he didn't seem to notice. For that small favor, Eden was most grateful.

"Who the hell else would I want?"

He was hurting. Eden knew the worst of his frustration was born, not of pain or even grief, but of a sense of utter helplessness. Men of Adams Cade's sort, men of action and daring and unique accomplishment, couldn't bear being helpless. Because he couldn't, perhaps he did need company.

Perhaps he even needed her—an old friend from the past. But even in his need, Eden knew instinctively that the last thing he would tolerate was sympathy.

"Who else would you need?" Tapping a manicured nail on linen, she pretended to consider the problem. "Ah," she murmured as if a solution had just occurred. "I have it."

"What do you have other than the will to drive me over the edge by repeating everything I say?" Adams' face was rigid and harsh. His temper hadn't abated. Nor did it seem any amount of coaxing would help.

But she could try. She would try. "It occurred to me that I might have Cullen call a lady of the evening." A delicate shrug lifted her shoulders, as she returned his heated look with an unruffled innocence. "I know it's morning, and the time frame wouldn't fit her job description, but surely he can find one who doesn't watch the clock. Except when...well, you know when.

"She might shock the neighbors and even the guests. But, after all, this is Fancy Row, the avenue of homes that sheltered wealthy, philandering planters' mistresses. It wouldn't be the first time a needy man turned to—''

''Dammit, Eden! Stop babbling.'' He'd spoken in a relatively low voice before, taking care not to disturb the diners beyond her quiet corner. Now his voice rose to an unmitigated roar. ''I don't need sex. But when I do, I can find my own. What I need this minute is *you*.''

Eden ignored the stares of startled guests. Risking one calm, reassuring glance for Cullen, who had abandoned his duties to watch Adams with chilling care, she questioned softly, ''You need me…as a friend.''

''Yes,'' Adams snapped.

''For my sweet, gentle voice of reason.''

''Yes, again.''

''You're sure you wouldn't rather have a lady?'' She shouldn't tease. She knew she shouldn't, but she couldn't resist.

''You are a lady.''

''Why, thank you, Adams. I didn't think you'd noticed.''

Ignoring her, he turned away, glaring across the room at the river visible beyond windows framed by clusters of ancient live oaks. ''Are you coming?''

Her look was innocent, masking the fact that she couldn't look away from him. Even frustrated and bristling and still a bit too properly dressed, he was magnificent. ''Coming where?''

''With me.'' Half turning, he looked about him grimly, as if he couldn't bear another minute trapped within confining walls. Poised to flee the massive, vaulted ballroom Eden had so skillfully converted into a dining room, he muttered bleakly, almost to himself, ''Please, Eden.''

Eden's lashes fluttered to her cheeks, hiding the hurt and the sparkle of tears in her eyes. This was Adams, once the reasonable peacemaker, slow to anger, quick to forgive. Adams, who hurt so badly he had lost the slow, easy smile and the infectious grin she loved. Adams, who needed *her*.

"Yes."

"I'm sorry I've been rude. I'm sorry I was angry. If I've offended you... What?" Adams interrupted himself abruptly. "What did you say?"

"I said yes," Eden repeated softly. "Yes, I'm coming with you." Wondering where her sense of self-preservation had gone, next she heard herself asking, "Where would you like to go, Adams? The river? The beach? For a sail?"

"You choose."

He was in no mood for crowds, or strangers, or for chance encounters with curious old acquaintances. Or even to choose. She realized that completely. But she also realized that as vulnerable as she was, the last thing she needed was to be alone with Adams Cade. Today or any day. Not because she was afraid of him. She would never be afraid of Adams. Never! The person she must fear was Eden Claibourne.

"There's a place on Summer Island where another branch of the river flows into the sea," she heard herself say. Certain she'd suddenly lost her mind, she reached deeply within herself to resurrect the normally sensible, levelheaded businesswoman she'd been for all the rest of her adult life.

But even that most sensible, most levelheaded woman struggled for control against impossible odds. Even as the sensible Eden whispered dire warnings that the island would be virtually deserted and dangerous, the daredevil Eden of old was saying aloud, "With only six houses scattered over three miles of beach and most of them unoccupied this early in the season, we would hardly be caught in a crowd.''

''Sounds like a winner.'' He was only a little less gruff.

''We can take the launch or we can sail. Whichever you would like, Adams.''

''Fine.'' Now that she had agreed to spend time with him, he didn't care where they went or how they got there. Any place, any way would do, as long as there was a change of scenery and Eden.

Wisely choosing not to make an issue of his nonanswer, Eden asked, ''Have you eaten?''

''Merrie brought me a tray.'' Scowling, he lifted a dismissive shoulder. ''But no, I haven't eaten. I wasn't hungry.'' Which, translated, meant he couldn't face another meal alone.

Eden wasn't surprised by his lack of hunger. He was too restive to be anything but frustrated. ''Maybe you'll want something after a sail and a walk on the beach. I'll ask Cullen to have a picnic basket prepared while I change.''

Checking her watch, she judged her time. ''Both the basket and I should be ready in fifteen minutes.'' Giving her a minute or two in the bargain to ease Cullen's worries. ''I'll meet you at the boathouse then. All right?''

''Right.''

Eden almost smiled, for they'd switched from sounding like an echo to a good imitation of a broken record. Gathering up the paperwork that really needed her immediate attention, she headed for the hall and the stairs.

''Eden? You are coming back?''

Her heart skipped at the raw need in his voice. Pausing, not daring to glance back for fear she would go to him and take him in her arms, she murmured, ''I'm coming back.''

"Promise."

"I promise, Adams."

The *River Lady,* the inn's single-masted sloop, was ready. Adams had changed into khaki shorts and a collarless knit shirt and was pacing the dock when she hurried down the boardwalk.

"Sorry I'm late. Troubles," Eden explained. "A minor crisis in the kitchen. A lost order, meaning no pistachio crust for the baked red snapper tonight."

"So you improvised." Exhibiting surprisingly little sign of being disturbed by the delay, Adams took the heavily laden basket from her. Setting it aboard, he came to assist her.

"With almonds," Eden said, more for something to say than for Adams. Busy words, a pitiful sop for the apprehension that wouldn't be still.

"Good choice. Almonds always work." Catching her by the shoulder, not caring if there were pistachios, almonds or red snapper, Adams slid his palm down the length of her arm. "Ready?"

Nodding and suppressing a tremor, with her hand clasped securely in his, Eden bounded on board. Something she'd done without assistance more times than she could remember. But Adams was feeling helpless enough. If the observance of this small courtliness eased even a second of his frustration, what would it hurt if she played the lady to his gallant gentleman?

Desperately determined not to go where the truth of that question might lead, once she regained her equilibrium, Eden assumed the routine duties of crewman. Keeping her gaze from him, not daring to allow even a moment of admiration for his dark masculinity, she dealt skillfully and almost too diligently with lines and rigging.

Once the sloop was ready and all gear stowed away, Eden offered him the helm. First as a boy, then a teen and finally, briefly, as a young man, Adams had navigated this course regularly. So regularly he could have done it in his sleep. But through the years, battered by time and tide and the occasional hurricane, the river's path had altered. On a hand-drawn chart kept scrupulously current, Eden traced the best route, pointing out snags and shoals and nesting grounds.

Then, with all things in order and sails aloft, there was nothing for her to do but sit back and leave the navigation to Adams. Leaning on the coaming, her cheek resting on her folded arms, she watched the river and Adams, hoping the changes in the channel would offer the challenge he needed.

At first there was a sense of ferocity in him. An intensity that made him impatient and awkward. A silent anger that knotted his shoulders and set his teeth grinding with the force of a vice. Once he'd played the current like a virtuoso, now he fought its quirks, rather than used them. He was a man at war, not the man who loved the sea.

Eden watched and hurt for him. There were times she yearned to help, to advise or make suggestions. But even on the verge of despair, she said nothing.

He was like a long-distance runner learning to walk a rutted road when what he wanted and needed was to race the wind.

For a while bitter impatience continued to defeat him. Then the ferocity faded. Intensity ebbed. Teeth unclenched and muscles began to flow in perfect coordination beneath the smooth, dark skin.

Gradually, with the return of remembered skills, the river and the subtle tranquillity of sailing worked their magic. The restlessness gathered within him like a wild tumult slowly quieted. Impatience turned to resolution, awkwardness to agility. Adams' love for the savannahs, the tidelands and the sea was reborn.

For Eden, watching the transformation was like stepping back in time. If only for a little while. If only for this day.

He didn't speak. Neither did she. But it became the silence of peace, of old friends reliving treasured times. Once he pointed out an eagle high above the river on the loneliest part of the channel. Eden remembered there had been no eagles in this part of the low country when he'd been taken from her. But fearful of breaking the spell, she would wait for another time to explain that now nearly a dozen of the majestic birds hunted the river.

There were other sightings. Deer with new fawns. Turtles sunning on limbs jutting above the surface of the river. Gators, as still as carved images, lying in wait for careless prey.

Even a shy wood stork posed for his pleasure. The gangly, comical bird was followed by grace personified—a flock of egrets, shining in the sun like polished ivory.

With each discovery, Eden saw his pleasure mounting, the troubles of his mind easing. Minute by minute the rigid perfection he'd worn like a shield was easing. And Eden knew that no matter what it might hold for her, she would never regret this journey.

They were moving smoothly now. Soon the channel broadened as it spilled into the estuary. In deeper water, as billowing sails caught the sea breezes, the *River Lady* sped along almost unattended. And Adams relaxed for the first time in years.

Nothing had changed. His father was still desperately ill, he was still an ex-con, still a disgrace to his family, and it was still likely he would never see Belle Reve again. He knew he couldn't forget, but he could ignore the heartache for the duration of the sail.

With a what-the-hell grin, he shucked his shirt, drew a ball cap from the back pocket of his shorts and angled it low over his forehead. Daring the wind to sweep it away, grasping the wheel again, he set the final course for Summer Island.

As the *Lady* skimmed through the surf, at starboard miles of calm, empty sea stretched endlessly, with distant white caps gleaming against an azure horizon. Port side, barrier island after barrier island slipped by with white sand sparkling like snow and jutting dunes overgrown with swaying sea oats.

One by one the sloop skimmed along their shores. One by one it passed them by, until they lay in the wake like a string of jewels.

Adams recalled that there were sixty-odd charted islands scattered along the coast bordering the outskirts of Belle Terre. Some were inhabited. Most were not. If tide and storm surges had been kind, Summer Island would be among the larger land masses.

With the tarnish of grief and guilt falling from his eyes, for the first time Adams realized that in the low country, spring had begun the first of its evolution into summer. In a matter of a week, the sun was brighter, the days warmer. The sea was bluer, the colors of the earth more intense. In salt-laden breezes whipping the sails and teasing his skin, there lay the whispered promise of lazy summer days to come.

"If only…" he murmured, then shook away the ache of nostalgia. He wouldn't be here in summer, when the days moved like warm, sweet honey, and the nights were magic in indigo. He couldn't be. But he wouldn't let regret for what he couldn't have destroy what he had.

What he had was this day. A day with Eden and the promises of a lady called Spring.

There was tranquillity in her promises, and with them a contentment that was contagious. All he was feeling was in the exuberance of the smile he flashed over his shoulder at Eden. And in the silent invitation in the hand he extended to her.

Mesmerized, Eden had watched him throughout their journey. Now the transformation was complete. He'd emerged from the shell that surrounded him like a marvelous animal waking from a pain-filled sleep. And, God help her, he was still so wickedly charming her heart hadn't a chance of surviving him intact.

Seeing Adams like this was more than she'd dared to hope for and all she feared. Yet, when his hand closed over hers, drawing her before him, Eden wished desperately this day would never end, that he could always be like this.

"Do you remember?" he asked against her cheek as his body fit closely with hers.

"The summer you taught me to sail?"

"Mm-hmm." He laughed softly. "Of all the musketeers, you were my best pupil."

"That's because I was your oldest pupil, Adams. Also, because you cut me some slack because I was the smallest."

"You were a little thing then. But not anymore."

"I grew."

"I'd say so." Adams chuckled. "In all the right places."

"Okay, smarty," Eden drawled. "I'm talking inches."

"So am I, sweetheart. So am I."

Eden searched for a snappy comeback, but before her

befuddled mind could manage one, as the sloop passed an uninhabited cay, Summer Island came into view.

The next few minutes were spent tacking along the riverside of the island to the first in a scattered row of docks dotting the bank. Securing the sloop went smoothly and quickly. Adams was first on the dock, then he turned to her with the courtesy she'd once expected and had come to expect again.

"Summer Island hasn't changed much," Adams observed as they strolled side by side along the boardwalk from the dock, past the house, then to the shore. *"Sea Watch,"* Adams read the name etched into a piece of drift. "Who lives here?"

"Friends. Recent friends—no one you would know. Devlin O'Hara bought this house a few years ago. It was a belated wedding gift for his wife, Kate."

"He loves her," Adams asserted, staring up at the massive structure of *Sea Watch.* A house that was perfect in its surroundings. A house as lovely as any he'd ever seen anywhere in the world.

"It took them a while to admit it, but I've never seen two people more in love. I'd like you to meet them, but they won't be back for a while yet. Their daughter, Tessa, is deaf, but there's new hope she might hear."

"They've gone to check it out?" Adams asked, but he knew the answer before Eden replied.

"Devlin would move heaven and earth for Tessa."

"I'd like to meet them someday. To thank them for the use of their island, if nothing else."

Long before the conversation ended, long before they reached the sandy beach, the whisper of the surf surrounded them. The tide was out, the sea was calm. Swimming in the salty water would be no more difficult than swimming in a lake.

They were ankle deep in the warming water when Eden cast off the terry-cloth sundress that covered her swimsuit. "Race you," she challenged, and splashed deeper into the tide. "First one to China wins."

Then she was gone from his sight, her body slicing through the water like a dolphin. Adams delayed only long enough to rescue her dress from the threat of a changing tide. He'd brought no suit, but this wouldn't be the first time he'd swum in his clothes. Or in nothing at all.

Eden surfaced and, with a dare-you fling of her head, tossed her hair from her face and beckoned for Adams to join her. She didn't have to dare him twice. His golden-brown body arced through the air, the sun and the sea like a knife. Three powerful strokes and he surfaced at her side. But before he could catch his breath, she was gone again.

For a time they played the game the way they had as kids. Tagging, diving, skimming the sandy bottom of the sea, riding the swells of the surf with one in pursuit of the other. Then, trading tags and doing it all again.

Until at last, instead of tagging her, Adams caught her in his arms. Holding her scantily clad body close, he brushed her hair back and leaned near as if to whisper a great secret. "Still want to try for China?"

"China?" Catching the glint in his eyes, Eden laughed. "So that's what this was about. Tiring me out so you would get there first. No fair."

"Does that mean you forfeit?" He grinned then, and it was the grin Eden remembered. The one that always swept the breath from her.

"You planned this," she accused. "Planned to exhaust me so I had to forfeit."

"Who tagged who…whom first?" He countered. "You did, sweetheart, so how does that make me a cheat?"

"Okay. Okay. A forfeit, then." With a mock glower, she demanded, "What do you want?"

"A kiss." Adams was as startled as she. He didn't know until now that he'd intended to kiss her. But when he was honest, he knew he'd wanted and needed her kiss for days.

"Just one," Eden warned as the beat of her heart matched the rush of the sea.

"Just one," Adams promised. But when he drew her to him, his strong body a caress against the slenderness of hers, both knew in their hearts that his promise was empty words. One kiss for lovers too long apart would never be enough.

"Adams…" Faltering, she linked her arms around his neck and leaned her forehead against his bare chest.

"It's okay, love. It was just a kid's game, and foolish. You don't have to—"

Her head came up, her bright gaze locked with his. "I do. God help me, Adams, I do."

"Are you sure, sweet Eden?" he whispered hoarsely. "Please be sure."

As she let the surge of the tide lift her to him, her breasts brushed his chest and her lips skimmed his. Once, twice, three times, before he groaned and caught her hard against him, before his mouth ground down on hers, before her lips parted, taking his tongue, meeting its caress with a caress of her own. Touching his body as he touched hers. Wanting him, needing him. Loving him.

With each touch he kissed her again and again. And with each she responded. And all the while, as they were lost in one another, the tide nudged them gently toward shore.

When Adams' feet brushed the tumbling sand, surf swirling around them, he caught her in his arms. He didn't ask again. All his questions had been answered.

There was a gazebo hunkered in the sand where shore and dunes melded, but he remembered glimpsing a deck with a chaise. One, no doubt, other lovers found convenient in their urgency.

From the boardwalk he moved to the stairs, but Eden's weight was as nothing. On the sun-scoured deck, he set her down, bent on stripping her like the madman she'd made of him. But Eden was there first. Like witchcraft, a flick of her wrist and the bandeau slipped from her breasts. Another flick at the left, then the right side of her bikini, and the last scrap of fabric that hid her from him slipped away.

She was so beautiful, needing no forgiveness from the unforgiving light of midday. So beautiful that he couldn't spend the time he wanted to woo her, to worship her. So beautiful that all he could do was draw her down with him to the chaise.

From that moment, the day became a blur. Adams never knew when he left her to shed the last of his clothing. From the moment she took his hand, bringing him back to her, back to her waiting body, he only remembered muttering, "Are you protected?"

Her stuttered, hesitant answer, "N…yes," rang in his mind like a godsend, then was forgotten as he drove deeply within her. Then nothing mattered but the healing balm of her welcoming softness, her heat. And finally, the sweet shudders that racked her body in harmony with his.

Four

——

His touch woke her.

The brush of his fingertips though the tangle of her hair drew Eden from a deep sleep. "Better wake up, sweetheart."

Her lashes were heavy on her cheeks, her body languid and far too comfortable to move. She sighed and stirred, and Adams' low chuckle drifting over her was as beguiling as his touch.

"You're like a kitten, soft and purring," he murmured hoarsely, the memory of her gentle cries as he made love to her forever branding his heart and mind. Looking at her now, curled beneath the beach sheet he'd scavenged from the sloop, it took every ounce of his resolve not to take her back in his arms. Even as every particle of wisdom he'd ever claimed, or thought to possess, argued that he mustn't make love to her again, he wanted her so badly he could barely restrain himself.

Adams knew, then, that he would have loved her. Against every reason, except the day had passed too rapidly, and now the angle of the sun had moved beyond the small circle of shade the umbrella he'd opened over her had provided. The gaily patterned shelter had served its purpose for a while. But now even it couldn't protect Eden from the slanting, burning rays.

As he watched her sleep, he realized that beyond the thin tan lines left by a garment no larger than a G-string, her body bore no marks of pallor. Eden's skin was a virtually flawless golden-brown. Certainly not the darkness of a compulsive sun worshiper, but neither was she a stranger to bathing naked or nearly naked on the beach. The image of her frolicking on some sandy shore, with only the sun, the wind, the sand and nearly nonexistent tiny threads to cover her, almost defeated his faltering resolve.

What lonely shore had she graced with her bare loveliness? he wondered. And had it truly been lonely?

Anger gripped him. Anger that another man might have seen her as he had, touched her as he had. Made love to her as he had.

Was there a lover? Did she wake like this for him, languid and content? With a look and a touch, did he want her again? Take her again, in the sun, in the sand, in the surf?

Adams' hands had curled into fists when he realized he hadn't the right to question. Or the right to be angry. What did he know about Eden? Who had she been? Who was she now? Who, more than Eden Claibourne, widow, innkeeper, old friend?

He had to know. His right to question or not, he must. "Eden," he coaxed softly. "Time to wake up. If we don't get you out of this sun, you might turn into a cinder.''

''No.'' Like the kitten, she purred and stretched. Her lashes fluttered, revealing a dreamy gaze. The towel slipped from her breasts and caught at her hips, but she didn't care. For this day, decorum had been cast to the wind and the sea. She wouldn't be coy; she was too honest to pretend. ''Not a cinder.'' A lazy note was in her voice. ''But a starveling for sure.''

''You're hungry.'' So was Adams, but not for food.

''As a bear.''

Considering his lecherous mood, and despite all determination to the contrary, Adams suspected that in the course of the remaining hours of the day, she would need all her strength. He offered the obvious remedy. ''I brought the basket from *Lady*. We can dine in the gazebo and take a break from the sun.''

''We could go in the house,'' Eden countered. ''I have a key. When Kate and Devlin are away, I check on the house and grounds.''

''Is that often?''

''No. Once Devlin O'Hara was a wanderer, but loving Kate and Tessa has tethered him contentedly in one place. Now both he and Kate are taking courses at the college. And both do quite a lot of volunteer work with children who have hearing problems.''

''Because of their daughter, Tessa?''

''Yes.'' Eden stood, dragging the towel with her. Folding it around her body, she tucked the ends securely over her breasts. ''The gazebo or the house?''

''The gazebo,'' Adams said after a hesitation. Not because he was unsure of his choice, but because his thoughts still dwelt on Eden and deserted beaches. Which beach? Where? With whom?

He was becoming obsessed with wondering.

"You hate it, don't you?" she asked him in a quiet voice.

Adams caught a startled breath, wondering if she'd read his thoughts or if he was that transparent.

"You need to be outside because you hate being cooped up," Eden suggested before he could respond or question. "That's part of why you were so restless this morning, isn't it?"

"That's part of it." It was a part of the truth, if not the strongest factor. He hated being confined. After years locked away in a prison, Adams had come to accept that he always would.

Satisfied by his sketchy agreement, Eden shifted her attention to the basket. When her hand collided with his, she looked up to find his seething gaze on her. Misinterpreting his turmoil, she touched his face, stroking the harsh lines that bracketed his mouth. "I understand what it's like to feel closed in, Adams. I know that even friendly walls can be confining.

"After my husband died and I came back to Belle Terre, it was a long time before I lost that caged feeling."

"You weren't in prison." His voice held no rancor, no hint of the questions her comment provoked.

"Not like you mean. There were no bars and no guards. In fact, the opposite was true. But that's ancient history. A story I'm sure you wouldn't find interesting." Eden took her hand from the basket. From the warmth of his touch, which made her deliciously aware of much more recent history. One they shared. "For now we should think of the present. And that's Adams Cade, Eden Claibourne, Summer Island and Cullen's basket."

She laughed huskily, the sound quiet, enticing. "The gazebo awaits, and I'm starved."

* * *

"As head steward, Cullen is a miracle." Adams finished the last strawberry, then the last sip of champagne, and slid his plate and the fragile flute away. "Where did you find him?"

"You could say I inherited him," Eden explained. "Cullen's family has been with my husband's family for more than a century. Nicholas and he were both the last of their line. When Nicholas died, in Cullen's mind, he became mine."

"The honor of old family traditions, sustained by love." Adams had known men like Cullen. "It's all he's ever known, and without someone to take care of he would die."

Eden's face was veiled in sadness. "After Nicholas' death, I couldn't stay on Fatu Hiva. It seemed obscene to stay in his Pacific paradise. But the island was Cullen's home. I thought he would be happier there. He was adamant in his refusal. Finally, I realized Cullen couldn't stay without Nicholas any more than I could."

"He's adjusted to the cultural differences?"

"Perfectly. But it really wasn't such a difference. He'd always traveled with Nicholas. And though wines became his passion and his specialty here, he does everything. Cullen even oversees the planning and planting of the gardens." Eden smiled now. "Though he does mourn the lack of orchids and ylang-ylang."

"Nicholas Claibourne of Fatu Hiva," Adams mused aloud. "The Marquesas archipelago and the Pacific Ocean are both a long way from the Atlantic and Belle Terre."

"You're wondering how Nicholas and I met."

"A man of such an exotic life—isn't it natural I would?"

"It was nothing dramatic. We were classmates at the

university. Nicholas came to study art and design with a visiting professor. I was in the same class. He was older, his education delayed by illness. We were drawn to each other. But when the class was finished, Nicholas returned to Fatu Hiva.''

''But he came back for you.'' Adams watched her in the shadows of the gazebo, imagining the vibrant young woman she would have been. Was it any wonder that a man with the soul of an artist would want her?

''I didn't see or hear from him for a year. In that year my grandmother and grandfather died within months of each other. When I graduated, I thought no one cared. Then I looked up, and Nicholas was there.''

''He'd come for you.'' Adams grieved that he couldn't have been there for her. When she lost her grandparents, the only family she'd ever had. When she graduated with honors. He'd wanted to hate the wealthy, worldly Nicholas Claibourne. Instead, he was grateful for the kindness of a man he'd never known.

''He asked me to marry him, to come with him to Fatu Hiva. There was nothing for me here anymore, so I said yes.''

Adams had listened to every nuance of every word. There was affection in her voice when she spoke of her husband and his exotic land. But Adams caught a hint of another emotion lying beneath the surface.

Eden spoke as if she'd been happy with Nicholas Claibourne, happy in his land. Yet not enough to stay. When he was gone, she had come home to Belle Terre. Adams wondered why.

''Did you love him, Eden?'' he asked softly.

There was sadness again, in her voice, in her eyes. ''As much as he wanted me to.''

Before he could question the cryptic remark, she was

clearing away their meal. A repast better suited for a gala than an impromptu picnic. But Eden had assured him that such was the masterful hand of Cullen. The chef at River Walk was famous now, and the dining room was always filled to overflowing because of his talent. But before he fell under the tutelage of Cullen Pavaouau of Fatu Hiva, he was only a cook.

"If you're ready for a walk, there's someone I'd like you to see." Eden had begun this journey thinking Adams needed quiet, with no strangers. But the man she spoke of was far from a stranger. "It isn't a great distance, and he would never judge you. He's probably lonely about now, with Tessa and Kate and Devlin away."

Summer Island was a gated community. A single guard watched over the privacy of six homes spaced over three miles of shore. Not a taxing task, but solitary. She rarely came to the island without stopping at the gatehouse for a visit.

"You want to tell me who this lonely person is?" Adams asked suspiciously.

"Nope." She shook her head, sending her hair flying in a rich cascade about her bare shoulders.

"You're going dressed in a towel?" Adams interest was definitely rising.

"He's seen me in less."

"He has, has he?" His first thought was that this was the lover with whom she sunned and played half-naked. His second thought was to doubt his first.

Eden had no other lovers. She was too honest, too innocent, to entertain more than one lover. He was sure of it. Without realizing when or how, Adams had come to trust Eden, the woman, as he had Robbie, the lonely tomboy.

The denial echoed in his mind. If there was another

man in her life, she would never have made love with him.

"Indeed, he has. I'm thankful it was him." Sadness had flown from Eden. Now her smile was natural and unforced.

"One wonders why," Adams mused.

"When you see him, you'll know."

By Adams' calculations, the walk to the gatehouse was less than two miles. If this innovation wasn't exactly at the midpoint of the landmass, it didn't miss by far. Their way had been meandering and filled with interruptions, as he lingered here and there to marvel at the changes.

"When we came here as kids, there were only two homes. Now there are six. But given the surge in buying and selling coastal properties, I suppose it's good fortune there are only six."

"McGregor is responsible for preserving the island as it is," Eden said as she scuffed along in heated sand, enjoying the familiar rasp of it against her toes and heels.

"McGregor, king of low-country asphalt?" Adams looked down at her as she strolled by his side. Contrary to her teasing, she'd slipped into the terry dress he'd rescued from the tide.

"He may be king of asphalt, but he fought hardest to ban it on Summer Island. In fact, he sees to the maintenance of the old shell path that winds through the dunes and along the shore."

"It traverses the length of the island as it always did?" The path of shells—or road of shells, as some called it— was one of the attractions that had drawn Adams and his brothers to the island in the few lazy days of summer Gus allowed them. Though most of the houses were fairly new by area standards, the path had meandered among the dunes for as long as anyone could remember.

Scholars touted it as the work of ancient natives. Perhaps the Chicora, who were known to congregate on the beaches as early as the sixteenth century. To hunt, to fish, to gather the plentiful oysters, clams and mussels.

A number of shell rings built of their rubble still survived centuries later. Even as a boy playing pirates and Indians on this lonely shore, Adams had wanted to believe the path was a part of that history. He wanted to believe it now.

"It remains the only thoroughfare reaching from one tip of the island to the other," Eden explained. "McGregor fought the only plan for a modern road, and he tends the old one with the greatest care. An unusually high or rough tide, or a hint of a storm, and he's here with his crew, making the necessary repairs."

Scooping up a sand dollar, she dropped it in the pocket of her dress. "The shell base must be quite deep, in all the years I've been back in Belle Terre, his repairs have been minimal. Accretion along the shore hasn't hurt in that respect."

"Who decided there would be only six houses?" Adams asked as he caught her hand in his. "Dare I suggest McGregor?"

Eden was breathlessly aware of her palm nestled in his and of the gentle strength in the fingers that held hers willingly captive. The same strength that had borne her to the deck of *Sea Watch*. The gentleness that had guarded his lovemaking.

Caught in her reverie, she lost the thread of conversation. But his clasp tightening drew her back to the present. As he led her past a fallen palmetto washed from another shore, she remembered Adams' question. "When an investor known for overdeveloping properties started poking around the island, McGregor swooped in and bought all the available land on both sides of the river. Then, with a plan for the preservation of the island, he began a limited development of his own.''

''A very limited and preserving development, indeed,'' Adams observed. ''Only six houses scattered over three or more miles of beach, with a ferocious, mysterious guard at the gate.''

Eden chuckled at Adams' description of the guard. ''I'll tell him you called him ferocious. It will make his day.''

''Not exactly Arnold Schwarz-his-name, I take it?''

''Hardly,'' Eden agreed. ''But he's quite good at his job.''

Pulling her hand from his, she dashed to the water's edge. Once again she caught a shell tumbling in the surf. After inspecting it carefully, she held it out to him. ''Perfect.''

The perfect find was an angel wing, both arcing shells still attached by the fragile membrane. A rare find, looking exactly like the lost wings of a tiny angel.

''A beauty,'' Adams murmured with scarcely a glance at her treasure. For *she* was the beauty, her face alight with the pleasure of her discovery. As she stood with the surf swirling about her ankles, a breeze that traversed the shore from land to sea molded the terry fabric of her dress to her. In the subtle swirl, the sensible garment became as provocative as the most revealing satin or lace. It didn't help Adams' physical state one bit to remember that beneath the cloth clinging to the rise of her breasts and the line of her hips and thighs, she was as naked as the image he carried in his mind.

God help him, he was two men in one where Eden was concerned. There was the irrational one, who thought only of his own needs. Who wanted to tear the dress from her that he might see her, every splendid inch, leaving nothing to be imagined. The madman who wanted to touch her, caress her and bear her down with him to the surf, in the sand, as if it was the first time.

And there was the man of reason, who struggled against his desire and the lust that burned like a flame. A man who realized there was no future for Eden with him. She was too civilized for a hardened ex-con. Too fragile for a brief affair with a man without a home. A man exiled from all he loved.

Yet every argument the reasonable side of Adams Cade offered, none had kept him from making love to her. None kept him from wanting her now.

"Dammit, Adams Cade, you made love to her once before and left her. This time can be no different." The condemning curse was muffled by the whisper of the surf. "Think of what's best for her. Twice was twice too much. Don't make it a third time, or a fourth."

"I'll leave this here while we make our visit, then pick it up on the way back to *Sea Watch*." Eden laid the shell carefully on the palmetto. Unaware of his muttered turmoil, her smile was tender. "This will be the best of my collection. You're my lucky charm, Adams. It was because of you that I found it."

"I'm not anybody's good luck," Adams denied shortly. "Especially not yours."

"You're angry." The light in Eden's gaze faded.

He took her hand back into his, wishing he could undo so many things. Wishing he was a different man, a better man. The man Eden thought him. "I'm not angry. At least not at you."

"Then what's wrong?" Had he remembered that in mutual and wild sexual need she'd stumbled over his question of protection? She wanted to explain about Nicholas. She needed to explain her strange, tragic marriage—and the mindless, unthinking risk a woman who might be barren had taken today in a moment of ecstasy.

But not on a day that had been all she'd dreamed a day with Adams could be. Surely the truth could wait.

"Nothing's wrong. Just a mood." He strove for a contrite grin. "I do have them, you know. As recently as this morning, if you'll remember."

"A mood." Doubt scored her face. "And you aren't angry."

"Never at you." Looping an arm around her, he drew her to his side. Burying his lips in her windblown hair, he whispered, "Let's put this behind us, visit your friend and go home."

Home. A word Adams avoided. Eden wondered if he was aware he'd called Belle Terre, even River Walk, the forbidden name.

Hoping that was a sign he'd grown comfortable there with her, Eden wrapped an arm around his waist. Nestled within his embrace, she walked with him to the bridge.

"Quite a structure." Adams paused between the rambling lawns of the houses flanking the entrance to the island. Except for the view from a few docks on the riverside, this was the best perspective of the bridge. "Not exactly what I expected."

"Everyone who owns a house here lives in Belle Terre. Some come by car, some by launch. Most sail. No one wanted the hassle of a drawbridge. So..." Eden indicated the handsome combination of steel and concrete embellished by carvings of stone. "On misty days it looks like a fairy's path, beginning and ending in clouds. The gatekeeper's cottage is small, but as well-done."

"So the mystery man lives in comfort?"

"As comfortable as he can be." Leaving Adams to interpret her comment as he would, Eden led him onto the bridge.

At the highest point of the arch he stopped her. Looking down on the swiftly moving current, he asked, "Do you remember when we jumped off the old wooden bridge that stood here?"

"And ended up knee-deep in silt?" Leaning against a stone figure, Eden looked back at the island. "That was the first time you let me come with you. Jumping from the bridge was a test. To scare me off."

"Nothing scared Robbie, did it?"

"I was scared. I just wouldn't show it."

"And now, Eden?"

"Hello, on the bridge." The voice, soft and Southern, but laced with the ring of authority, cut neatly through his question.

The elderly man hobbled toward them. "Eden, is that you?"

"Yes, Hobie." She faced the guard. "I've brought someone to see you."

The old man lurched forward a pace, his faded gaze peering, when Adams said in fond recognition, "Hello, Mr. Verey."

"Adams?" Hobie took another step. "Adams Cade?"

"Yes, sir. Adams."

"Well, damn boy." Hobie grabbed the hand Adams offered, pumping it vigorously. "It's about time you came home."

"This isn't home, Mr. Verey. Not anymore," Adams said as Hobie stepped back a pace. "I've only come for a visit."

"Whatever your reason, it's good for these old eyes to see you." Hobie shrugged away Adams' explanation.

"Come on over to the gatehouse for a real visit. I've just made a brand-new pitcher of lemonade. Too much for me, since Tessa's not here."

The old man didn't wait for an acceptance. He simply stumped away, as if he never doubted Eden and Adams would follow.

"Once you spoke, I knew it was you. Would have known it blindfolded. None of the boys but the Cades called me Mister. It's a known fact none of the Cades would be mistaken for each other." With a sigh, Hobie leaned his hunched, arthritic back against the faded upholstery of his lounge chair.

Drawing an easing breath, he spoke with renewed vigor. "No siree, I don't think I've ever seen four brothers so different or so alike. In some ways Gus did good by you boys. In most he was a damned fool."

Adams and Eden listened, sipping lemonade and nibbling chocolate-chip cookies Kate O'Hara had baked. They said very little as Hobie Verey rambled and reminisced.

The old man was lonely and he was very fond of Adams.

"I always knew there was something fishy about the night Junior Rabb got his skull cracked. Not your style, Adams. In all your brawling days, you never hit a man from behind. A dozen witnesses would testify to that. But you never said a word, did you? Not one word in your own defense during the whole trial."

Slowing for another breath, then taking a sip of lemonade, Hobie patted Adams' knee. "Mayhap, now that you're home, you can spend some time setting the record straight."

"There's nothing to set straight, Mr. Verey," Adams

said. "It was set straight as it needs to be thirteen years ago."

Hobie Verey turned a suddenly keen and piercing gaze on Adams. "You mean as straight as you want it to be, don't you?"

"No, sir." Adams put his lemonade aside. "I meant it exactly as I said it. Everything about that night is as straight as it needs to be." His voice softened. "But I thank you for your confidence and trust, however misplaced it is."

"Ain't a case of misplaced trust," Hobie said as softly. "Just another Cade too stubborn for his own good. You need to stay, do what's right for yourself and this little girl."

Looking over the spectacles he'd perched on his nose when they'd come inside the cottage, he sent a stern look at Eden. "Now that you're older and, I hope, wiser, I assume you choose more suitable places than my favorite fishing hole to go skinny-dipping."

Eden laughed, even as she blushed. "Now that I know which is your favorite, I do."

Hobie's spectacles slipped lower as he raised his brows. "Impudent chit. I suppose that means you do still skinny-dip."

"Every chance I get." Eden had left her chair. She leaned over Hobie to kiss his balding head. "Every single chance I get."

"Then I suggest you beware of this scalawag."

"Oh, I will, Hobie. I will." Another kiss fell on his scalp. "Just not too much."

"That's good, then." Hobie didn't try to rise. He made no excuses to Eden for the lack of old-world courtesy once so much a part of him. She, better than most, understood his crippling arthritis. "Just remember, he's a good lad. No matter what folks say he's done or what blame he's taken, he's a good lad." Hobie's grimace was painful. "Gus Cade's a fool. Anyone else would welcome such a son home with open arms. No matter what he claims to have done." The old man's faded gaze turned piercing once more as it lifted one last time to meet Adams'. "Especially for what he claims to have done."

Adams said nothing for a moment as he stepped forward and laid a hand on the thin shoulder, so frail and misshapen beneath the immaculate uniform. "Thank you, Hobie. I'll never forget that you believed in me."

"Don't thank me for the truth." Shaking off the belligerence he used as a shield, as his farewell Hobie murmured, "Come back again, Adams. Before you go. If you go."

The walk back down the beach was subdued and silent, each lost in thought, considering Hobie's comments. By unspoken agreement and because the hour was growing late, together they gathered up their gear. And while Eden checked on the house, Adams stowed it away on the *River Lady*.

He was sitting at the helm, his face carefully without expression, when she jogged to the dock. The sloop was under sail and well on her way to the inn, when Eden spoke.

"You were always his favorite."

"Hobie?" Adams didn't look away from the channel as he navigated a tight turn. "I know."

"He's never thought you were capable of harming Junior Rabb unprovoked or provoked. He still won't."

"When a gentleman like Hobie Verey has a soft spot for someone, he never gives up."

"Neither do I, Adams." There were unanswered questions in her voice and in her eyes.

Questions, Adams knew, she wouldn't ask.

"I know," he murmured softly, and held out his hand to her.

When she twined her fingers with his, he pulled her close. She smelled of sea mist and sunshine. And underneath it, something exquisitely exotic, something he couldn't define but had come to accept as another enchanting part of her.

As he held her, breathing the mysterious scent, the terry sundress was as nothing beneath the caress of his fingertips. That she had come so naturally into his arms made him ache with need. Made him want to find a quiet cove, anchor the *Lady* just offshore and spend the night making love to her.

Yes, he'd made love to her already. And restraining himself at this late date didn't mitigate the sinfulness of his heedless greed. But he hoped one thoughtful, final abstinence would make the inevitable parting easier. At least for Eden.

Please, Adams prayed, at least for Eden.

The remainder of their journey was spent in a silent embrace. The sloop was making the last turn that would bring the inn into sight when he leaned toward Eden, his arms tightening about her as he whispered, "No matter what happens to me, no matter where I go, I'll never forget you, or this day."

Eden knew then that he wouldn't do as Hobie asked. As soon as the problem with Gus Cade health was resolved, no matter what the resolution, Adams would leave Belle Terre.

For Eden the air was suddenly cloying and damp. The threat of a gathering storm lay heavy in the night. And everything was changed.

Adams had been a gentle, considerate lover, but consummate and complete. She ached from head to toe. A sweet ache. A guilty ache. An added complication to his life. Eden couldn't believe what she'd done, that she'd been such a wanton. Teasing him, seducing him with the beguiling peace and contentment of Summer Island.

Had she planned this day? In her secret thoughts had she schemed to steal another passionate liaison to hold like a precious memory in her heart? Was creating a memory the worst of what she'd done?

Eden didn't know. She couldn't think. Doubt made her fearful of the truth and guilty for the complication she might have added to Adams' life. Yet beneath the guilt there was the bittersweet truth that, for a little while, Adams had loved her.

Nothing could take that away from her. Not guilt, not doubt. Adams would weather what he must, as he must, with the uncommon strength of a man who had been tested by fire. Then he would go. He would be safe. He would be free.

Eden would be left with a secret joy nothing could sully.

But as the *River Lady* negotiated the final twist of the channel and Adams guided her with an expert hand to the dock of the inn, a grim welcoming committee awaited them. One that swept both joy and guilt and dreams from her mind.

As her bleak gaze moved from the stony faces of Jefferson, Jackson and Lincoln, then finally returned to Adams, a shuddering wave of dark premonition descended over her.

"It's bad." She heard Jefferson say in a low and urgent voice as he reached from the dock to clasp Adams' outstretched hand. "He's asking for you."

Five

———

Belle Reve. *Beautiful dream.*

Drawing his horse to a halt at the end of an avenue of live oaks, Adams Cade looped the reins around his fingers and leaned on the pommel. As he looked around, he drew a deep breath, catching the scent of flowers. On a breeze, mingled with the familiar incense of the marsh and the river beyond, lay memories of stories he'd heard all his life.

The plantation was well named. It had been a dream, beginning with restless Jean Cadieu, who found the English rule of Barbados too stifling. Seeking more and better, the Breton joined an expedition led by William Hilton and was among the first to explore this land. The intrepid adventurer found beauty to match his dream in a world so enchanting he abandoned his wandering to claim a part of paradise.

Still young, still brash, with the last of a family fortune

he'd nearly squandered, Cadieu purchased every acre of land he could. When he couldn't purchase, he bartered. When he couldn't barter, he gambled. Amassing an estate no longer measured in acres, but in miles.

As his holdings grew, so did his wealth. As his wealth grew, so did his influence. Some called him a wise investor. Others called him scoundrel.

No matter what history recorded of his morals and deals, a dynasty was founded in the new world. And with it a new family name, as John Cade, once Jean Cadieu, begat progeny with the same verve he'd employed in acquiring his land. Through that land and his descendants, John Cade's legacy survived for centuries.

"Belle Reve," Adams murmured. Where he never expected to be again. At the end of the narrow, winding drive flanked by gnarled oaks, lay the manor. And Gus.

The old man had been sleeping when Adams arrived the night before. A welcome delay of the inevitable, as the brothers talked through the night. When the first of dawn flamed across the horizon, borrowing one of Jackson's Black Arabians, he'd ridden out to see for himself what their discourse revealed.

Though he'd seen his brothers in his week at the inn, until there was no recourse, neither had warned him of what he would find at Belle Reve. Nothing could have shocked him more than the reported state of the plantation's affairs.

A state, he could hardly believe, even though Jefferson assured him that when he spoke of the bad situation, he meant Belle Reve. Not Gus' condition. Yet Adams knew that none of his brothers would swear that one didn't go in hand with the other.

So, for Gus and for himself, sunrise found Adams riding the vast holdings of the Cade estate, seeing the decay, mourning the dereliction of years. But only three years, actually.

Three years since Gus had dismissed all the house staff and the crews that kept the place functioning. Many he'd let go had been born on the plantation, and the only home they'd ever known or wanted was Belle Reve. Some offered to stay, working just for the rent of their homes. Gus had been adamant.

One woman was allowed to stay to cook and clean, but only because Gus was alone. Lincoln was on the other side of the continent then, qualifying for advanced degrees in veterinary medicine. Jackson was in Ireland, specifically County Kildaire, learning the art of breeding the famed Irish horses.

That left the youngest to bear, again, the burden of being the favorite. Jefferson who, in his need for penance, coped with this madness for two years. The third year of deterioration, Gus' sons, all but the wicked eldest, had been home.

It was Jefferson he despaired for most. As the eldest, Adams had been Gus' verbal whipping boy. But compared to the guilt Jeffie felt for being the favored son, he knew long ago it was he who had the better of the bargain.

Drawing a long breath, Adams admitted that as harsh and demanding as Gus had been, he'd never asked less of himself. A trait that inspired loyalty and love, if not affection. The truth was, Lincoln, Jackson, Jefferson and even he would walk through fire for their father.

"But this isn't fire, Gus." Mentally Adams tabulated the problems. Fences rotting and falling down. Barns in dire need of new roofs and paint. Pastures once lush and green, overgrown by weeds and young saplings. Fields lying fallow. "I could put out a fire, but how do I rebuild a fallen empire when I'm not welcome until death comes knocking?''

The Arabian flicked his ears as if wondering why his rider waited at the end of a road, conversing with himself. Adams agreed he must look pretty silly, loitering at the most distant point of the drive as if space would give him courage.

Leaning forward, he stroked the neck of the handsome stallion. ''You're right, Blackhawk, this is silly. Putting off the inevitable only makes it worse. I've seen the destruction. Now it's time to face the ruler of our jungle.''

He looked frail in the morning light.

Adams had always thought of his father as a big man. In thirteen years, he seemed to have shrunk and drawn into himself. His right hand, paralyzed by his stroke, lay lax and useless on the arm of his wheelchair. A cup of coffee was gripped in the left. Only Gus' eyes hadn't changed. They still blazed with twin fires of eternal anger.

''Hello, Gus.'' Adams had stood in the archway leading to the breakfast room, watching the man he'd thought would never grow old struggle with a meal of only toast. He'd wondered how he would address his father. Now he discovered he'd thought of him as Gus too long to call him by any other name.

The chair whirred. In retreat, slender tires whispered over dusty tile. The cup was set with exaggerated care on a low table. The chair turned back. Snapping black eyes sunken in a pale face glared up at him. ''What the hell are you doing here?''

''You asked for me.'' After his first steps Adams had moved no farther into the room. ''Jefferson and Jackson and Lincoln came to The Inn at River Walk for me last night.''

"Last night!" The chair moved closer. Black eyes glared more brightly. "You were here last night?"

"Yes, sir. You were asleep when we arrived."

"'We'? I guess that means your brothers are here, too."

"Yes, sir." Adams held the burning gaze. "Jackson's seeing to the horses he boards with you. Lincoln's checking a mare that's about to foal. Jefferson has—"

"Gone hunting or fishing, or out to draw his pretty pictures, or wherever the hell else he's always running off to."

"Jefferson works hard, Gus. Jackson and Lincoln both say he does. Harder than one man should." At the moment the maligned youngest was trying to repair a rusted tractor that should have been junked twenty years before.

"You back-talking me, boy?" The chair lurched another foot closer. Then stopped so abruptly Adams feared the frail body of the man who was his father would be thrown to the floor.

He wanted to reach out, to steady the chair and the man. Instead, he said calmly, "No, sir. I'm just telling you the truth."

"I spoiled the boy," Gus grumbled.

If it hadn't been so sad, Adams would have laughed at the idea of Gus Cade spoiling anyone. "Maybe you weren't as hard on him as the rest of us, but Jeffie wasn't spoiled."

"No," Gus admitted grudgingly. "Guess not."

The chair whirred and spun. A tire squeaked and skidded. Adams called a warning he couldn't stifle. "Careful. You have the brakes set, Gus."

"Damn fool thing." The old man hit the arm of the chair with the heel of his good hand. A move that dislodged his right hand and set it swinging at his side like an untethered rope. Gus was slow to realize, but when he did, an awkward struggle of another sort began.

A struggle that, in spite of all Gus had said and done, almost ripped Adams' heart apart. Hands fisted, he stood his ground, fighting the anguish. Gus was tough. He'd survived more than he should have. He might survive anything this stroke threw at him. But never pity.

So Adams stood and waited, and prayed.

Reaching across his body with his good left hand, Gus clasped the wrist of the flaccid right arm. He'd almost lifted it to the arm of the chair when it slipped from his grasp to dangle again like a dead thing.

Once, twice more, he struggled with his arm. Twice more it slipped away. Finally he had no more strength and no more will for the struggle. Muttering a curse, he slammed back in his chair. His head dropped, his chin almost touching his heaving chest.

Gradually the panting of exertion eased. The slow rhythm of his breathing had returned when Gus lifted his head. He was pale, his eyes more sunken in their sockets. But the fire was still there as his gaze met Adams', and a silent message passed between father and son.

Giving no sign that Gus had asked for anything, Adams went to his father's side. Kneeling by the chair, he lifted the dangling arm and placed it gently on the chair.

Still kneeling, he hesitated. In that small hesitation he felt the brush of an unsteady hand over his hair. But when he looked at Gus, there was no sign that he'd touched him. And the good left hand lay in his lap.

Without speaking Adams stood. And Gus caught his hand.

"I asked you to come here..." Gus wasn't offering an apology for the years of exile. But whatever his reason for explaining, it was as difficult. Licking dry lips, he began again. "I asked you here to fix this. To fix Belle Reve.

"Lincoln knows trees and animals and their medicine. Jackson knows horses and breeding. Jefferson… You're right—he works hard. Harder than a man should. But you, Adams, you know numbers. You understand business. If anyone can straighten this out, you can."

"That's what this is about? All this?" A stabbing gesture indicated the view from an unwashed window. "It's about letting what you love more than anything in the world fall into ruin because of financial troubles? When I—"

"Don't want your money," Gus interrupted stubbornly. "I want your help."

"How?"

"Straighten out the books. See what's needed to set it all right financially. Then put it back in shape physically."

Adams couldn't believe what he was hearing. "You want me to go back to being a laborer?"

The words were hardly out of his mouth before Adams understood. Pride. Gus was too proud to let anyone see and know the condition poor management had wreaked on Belle Reve. To that end he would work his sons like animals. And, Adams admitted, the old rascal knew his sons would do exactly as he wished.

"All right." Adams backed away, a spark of hope for things he hadn't yet admitted dying inside him. "All right," he said again. "I'll do it, Gus Cade. I'll put your plantation in financial order. I'll repair what needs repairing. No matter how long it takes or what it takes, I'll do it—on one condition."

"What damned condition?" The old man bristled.

"That I have a free hand. No interference, no matter if you agree with what I do or not," Adams said in a tone only a fool would challenge. "No compromises, Gus. My way, or no way."

"Hellfire and damnation, you drive a hard bargain."

Adams didn't relent. "I had a good teacher."

He might not like the imposing of conditions, but Gus Cade was desperate and smart enough to know he had no choice. "All right. All right. I agree. No interference, no compromise."

"My way?" Adams repeated.

Gus stared out the window at some distant point. When Adams thought he wouldn't agree, he muttered, "Your way."

"I'll be back tomorrow morning. Seven sharp. I'll begin then." Turning on his heel, the exile of Belle Reve strode across the breakfast room.

"You can stay here," Gus called after him.

Adams halted, his shoulders tensing in his silence.

"Lincoln keeps a place in town. Says it's closer to his office and to the other farms if he's needed for a barn call. Jackson goes back to River Trace, the falling-down farm he thinks he can turn into a first-class breeder's farm." Gus' shrug dismissed the notion. Only one shoulder moved. "Jefferson does whatever it is Jefferson does in the evenings. But he'll always be along sometime in early morning."

A frown touched Gus' face. For the first time Adams realized the paralysis affected his expression. "Jeffie never slept a lot, Gus. You know that. He used to wander the swamps, hoping to catch some of the nocturnal animals prowling."

"Should've grown out of that by now." Gus' voice had taken on a petulant tone. He was tired. The conversation, the admission that he needed help, coupled with struggling with his arm, had taken a lot out of him.

''Jeffie told me you were released from the hospital with two nurses. Where are they? I've been here since last night, and I've seen neither hide nor hair of them.''

Gus chuckled at the familiar expression. ''They're hiding. I dared them within an inch of their lives to interrupt our little talk.''

''You were that sure I would be here?''

''Not today,'' Gus admitted. ''But I knew you'd be along.''

''You know me pretty well, it seems.''

''Well enough.'' Adams had moved as he spoke and Gus' chair turned with him. ''Well, enough, Adams Cade.''

''Then you know I won't sleep here, tonight or any night.''

Gus' shaggy eyebrows lifted a notch. ''Guess that means you'll be sleeping where you've been the past week.''

The old man had been gravely ill, his body ravaged and weak, but his mind was still sharp. ''By that remark, I assume you've heard I've been staying at The Inn at River Walk?''

Gus laughed, a caricature of his usual guffaw. ''Never assume. What I heard was that you were in Belle Terre. It wasn't any great mental stretch to figure where you were. Hell, boy, years ago a blind man could see you had a thing for the gal who turned River Walk into an inn.''

Still chuckling in a wheeze, the old man steered his chair to the table, took a sip of cold coffee and fixed his glare on Adams again. '''Pears you still do. Preferring her over blood kin.''

Blood kin. The term rankled. Especially when the man who called it up now like a weapon had announced to the world, those long and savage years ago, that Adams Cade was no longer any son of his and would never be welcome at Belle Reve again. But Adams knew he couldn't dwell on that. He couldn't let old wounds fester.

Despite Gus' rejection, he was here now, at Belle Reve. He'd said he would help and he would. On his terms.

"You're mistaken about Eden," he said into the silence. "I was too old for her."

"At twelve and seventeen, maybe. Even fifteen and twenty." A sly look crossed the ravaged face of Gus Cade. "Nineteen and twenty-four was a different situation, wasn't it?"

Adams barely silenced a startled gasp. The look he shot the taunting old man was fierce. But Gus was enjoying himself too much to care.

"Thirty-two and thirty-seven evens the odds that much more. Except, maybe, she's getting a little long in the tooth. The newfangled bio-log-ical clock women her age are moaning and groaning about," Gus added with a shake of his head.

"Not as new as you think." Adams was tired of sparring. His father seemed to thrive on it. "But you wouldn't know about that, would you? All your wives, four to be exact, were barely out of their teens. Maybe that's why none of them stuck."

"Not all of them left me," Gus defended himself with a satisfied look. He'd gotten a rise out of Adams, which meant the boy wasn't as cool toward Eden Claibourne as he pretended.

"No," Adams agreed. "My mother and Lincoln's worked themselves to death for you. Jackson's and Jefferson's mothers were smart enough to skip out on the drudgery." Realizing his hands were clenched, he opened his fists and flexed his fingers. "But you didn't care, did you? You had what you wanted. All you ever wanted from any of them.''

''Sons.'' Gus' left hand struck the arm of his chair. ''What any man wants. Sons to perpetuate his line.''

''Have you ever wondered what you would have done if we'd all been daughters? What then, Gus?''

''But you weren't,'' the old man countered. ''That's all that counts.''

''With you.'' Raking a hand across the back of his taut neck, Adams realized the toll of sleepless nights. ''If we're all done here, I have things to do.''

He was almost at the door when Gus called out, ''Give Miss Eden Claibourne my regards.''

''It's *Mrs.* Eden Claibourne, Gus.'' Then, with a shrug, he added, ''I'll be back tomorrow.''

''Damn,'' Adams swore harshly as he almost stumbled. He was tired. As tired as he could remember. Work detail in prison had never been like this. Even the oil rigs hadn't been like this. Only working for Gus had been this hard. Chuckling as he negotiated the darkened path leading to the river cottage, he muttered, ''Hell, this *was* working for Gus.''

You've grown soft, Cade, a voice in the back of this mind taunted. *Too many years sitting at a desk becoming the newest business sensation has turned you into a marshmallow.*

''Not quite.'' Adams flexed a stiffening shoulder.

He hadn't left after the confrontation with Gus. Instead, he'd rounded up his brothers for a family conference. Next he'd helped Jefferson with the tractor. By then, the foal was wobbling around the stall and his dam was on her feet. Finally, together, the four of them tackled the most critical projects.

Lincoln took an emergency call from a desperate dairy farmer and had to leave. But the three left worked past sundown.

Jackson had to leave to see to the stock he boarded with Gus. Then he had to return to River Trace to bed down the stock he kept there. Black Arabians at Belle Reve. Irish Thoroughbreds and Sport Horses, for the most part from the County Kildaire, at River Trace.

Jefferson skipped an art class to work as long as Adams.

Too long, Adams realized now. He was far too weary and ached too much to sleep, and tomorrow promised to be hell.

Tomorrow he would begin with Gus' books. Then, if he could, he would untangle the mess the old man had made of the financial affairs of Belle Reve.

But tonight, though he knew he wouldn't sleep for a while, he was determined not to think of Gus, or books, or Belle Reve. Adams Cade was determined not to think at all.

It was a measure of his weariness that he didn't notice the small torches dimly lighting his way down the winding path to the river cottage. A measure of his preoccupation that the exotic fragrance drifting from the lanai didn't warn him.

He was taken totally by surprise when he stepped into the shelter and found a candle flickering in a small hurricane lamp set in the midst of a tray of food too picturesque to eat. Yet too fragrantly delicious to resist.

Suddenly he was hungry, after all. Not ravenous, but in need of food. With a damp towel he found folded neatly by the tray, he wiped the sweat of his labor from his face and the dirt of Belle Reve from his hands. Tossing it aside and taking up the tray, he wandered to the edge of the lanai. Leaning against a column, while he watched the play of moonlight over the river, he devoured every morsel.

When the last of the fresh fruit steeped in a raspberry liqueur had disappeared, he sighed and leaned his head back against the column. "Thank God for Cullen. Silent, inscrutable, ever-present Cullen."

"Not Cullen this time." Eden moved from the shadows, from the seat she'd taken to wait for Adams.

"Eden." He said her name as if she were a part of heaven. Perhaps she was, he thought, as she moved into the light of the flickering lamp. The night was hotter than any in recent memory, and sultry. In keeping with the temperature, she wore a strapless sundress of a patterned fabric he didn't recognize. Her hair, usually so smooth and sleek, had begun to curl in the humid air. Not the wild, tousled curls of the young girl who lived in his memories, but the flamboyant disorder of a seductive woman.

"Eden," he said again as she moved closer, and the scent that enticed him when he was with her and haunted him when she was away enfolded him.

"Adams."

She said his name. Only his name, and every nerve, muscle and sinew forgot his fatigue. "I didn't know you were there. Were you waiting for me?"

"Yes."

Her soft answer sent whispers of desire swirling in the pit of his stomach. "It's after midnight. Have you waited long?"

"Not long." Brushing her hair from her face with her palm and letting her fingertips slip down her neck to the hollow of her throat, she lifted her gaze slowly to his. "Jefferson called me."

The Silhouette Reader Service™ — Here's how it works:

Accepting your 2 free books and gift places you under no obligation to buy anything. You may keep the books and gift and return the shipping statement marked "cancel." If you do not cancel, about a month later we'll send you 6 additional novels and bill you just $3.34 each in the U.S., or $3.74 each in Canada, plus 25¢ shipping and handling per book and applicable taxes if any.* That's the complete price and — compared to cover prices of $3.99 each in the U.S. and $4.50 each in Canada — it's quite a bargain! You may cancel at any time, but if you choose to continue, every month we'll send you 6 more books, which you may either purchase at the discount price or return to us and cancel your subscription.

*Terms and prices subject to change without notice. Sales tax applicable in N.Y. Canadian residents will be charged applicable provincial taxes and GST.

If offer card is missing write to: Silhouette Reader Service, 3010 Walden Ave., P.O. Box 1867, Buffalo NY 14240-1867

NO POSTAGE
NECESSARY
IF MAILED
IN THE
UNITED STATES

BUSINESS REPLY MAIL

FIRST-CLASS MAIL   PERMIT NO. 717   BUFFALO, NY

POSTAGE WILL BE PAID BY ADDRESSEE

SILHOUETTE READER SERVICE
3010 WALDEN AVE
PO BOX 1867
BUFFALO NY 14240-9952

GET FREE BOOKS and a FREE GIFT WHEN YOU PLAY THE...

Lucky 7

Just scratch off the silver box with a coin. Then check below to see the gifts you get!

SLOT MACHINE GAME!

YES! I have scratched off the silver box. Please send me the 2 free books and gift for which I qualify. I understand I am under no obligation to purchase any books, as explained on the back of this card.

326 SDL C4GV

225 SDL C4GR
(S-D-OS-08/00)

NAME (PLEASE PRINT CLEARLY)

ADDRESS

APT.# CITY

STATE/PROV. ZIP/POSTAL CODE

7 7 7	**Worth TWO FREE BOOKS plus a BONUS Mystery Gift!**
🍒 🍒 🍒	**Worth TWO FREE BOOKS!**
♣ ♣ ♣	**Worth ONE FREE BOOK!**
🔔 🔔 🍒	**TRY AGAIN!**

DETACH AND MAIL CARD TODAY!

"Oh." Adams' gaze was riveted on the bewitching path of her hands. He was only vaguely aware that the newest phenomenon of the business world couldn't manage anything more intelligent than a grunt. Nor could this phenomenon think of anything but that nothing could ever be more alluring than Eden in a sundress. Except Eden without a sundress.

Taking the forgotten tray from his hand, she set it on the table and returned to Adams. He realized then that she was barefoot and likely wore little or nothing beneath the soft, clinging fabric of her dress.

He didn't speak as she brushed his disheveled hair from his forehead. Or when her palm and fingers caressed his face and throat exactly as she had her own.

"You look tired. Jefferson warned me that you would be," she whispered, as if she would soothe him with her voice while her fingertips found the tight muscles at the curve of his neck and his shoulder. "You feel tired."

He laughed wearily and spanned her waist with his hands. "Other than Jeffie's tattling, how can you tell?"

"I feel it here." Before, she'd touched him with only one hand; now she lifted both to his face, and her touch sought his temples. In slow circles she massaged the ache left by tension and gritted teeth. "Our gruff Gus did a number on you."

"Yes." Adams discovered the word was slurred, his voice raw, as her intuitive exploration found new tensions to soothe.

"Eden," he managed as her hands slid from his shoulders, down his arms, then to his wrists to take his hands in hers. "I'm not sure this is a good idea."

She shook her head, and in candlelight her hair was like flyaway silk. One hand brushed over his lips, the fingers of the other laced with his. "Come with me," she said softly. "There's more waiting for you."

She led him to a small alcove off the side porch. The trellis that surrounded it was draped in vines of Carolina Jessamine. Its tiny white flowers filled the night with a perfume of its own.

Protected from the slight breeze by the cottage and the vines, more candles burned and danced. In the midst of the flowers and the bright flames sat an ornately carved tub of wood filled with water strewn with the petals of more flowers.

"What—"

Her hand over his mouth stopped him. "Trust me." Her voice was a melody. "You're weary and hurt, but if you give yourself completely into my care, before the evening is done, you won't remember heartache or fatigue.

"Will you trust me, Adams?"

Her touch was a caress that had become familiar. As her fingertips lingered again at his temple, he could only nod.

He didn't resist when she slipped the buttons of his shirt from their moorings. Nor when she slid the salt-encrusted garment from his shoulders and down his arms.

His breath stopped, his skin quivered as she stroked his body, but still he didn't resist. It was when her hands settled at the button at the band of his slacks that he protested. "No."

"Yes," she said firmly, but without raising her voice. "I've seen you naked, Adams. God willing, I will again. But this isn't about nakedness or sexuality. For now, it's about easing what hurts. Then the rest will go as it must."

Falling silent, she said nothing for a heartbeat, then, her gaze holding his, she whispered, "Please."

Slowly Adams' resistance faded. An outcast who

thought himself too hard for a gentle woman, he fell completely beneath her spell. And slowly Eden continued to undress him. When no garment remained, she led him to the tub. He expected she would join him—instead, she knelt to take up a coarse sponge. With soap and the sponge, amid the caress of floating flowers, she bathed him.

Adams couldn't remember a woman ever bathing him. Not even his mother. Only Gus. A Gus he remembered as being gentle. As gentle as work-worn callused hands could be.

Recalling lost memories of that father, gradually he relaxed. With one image slipping into another of a younger Gus laughing with his sons, working with them, driving himself harder than anyone, Adams drifted into restful, cleansing sleep.

Eden's voice calling his name brought him back to the lanai. Back to her. Obediently he rose, standing without shame as she dried him with a towel, impossibly rich, impossibly thick.

There was nothing erotic in her manner or in his response. Not even when she took him by the hand to lead him to the bedroom.

As the lanai and the alcove had been transformed, so had his bed. The coverlet and sheets had been stripped away. In their place lay a pad of the same luxuriant cloth as the towel. On the beside table sat a tray with a collection of bottles.

The pad was like a cloud when he stretched his lean frame across it. Eden's hands were no longer hands but instruments of magic as she stroked and kneaded taut muscle. What the meal and the bath had begun, her comforting touch nurtured. The gentle probe of her fingers found the last, deep clench of tension, the last secret tentacle of fatigue.

From head to fingertips to toes, she sought the demons of the body, while the soothing scent of her oils recalled peaceful images that eased his mind. Sure and tirelessly her hands glided over him until there was nothing but her touch and serenity.

Eden knew the moment he was completely at peace, completely beneath the spell she'd sought to weave. Adams was a strong man, a man of honor, a man who endured. But life had wounded him, and he wouldn't be whole until the wounds were healed. Eden hoped that in the serenity she had given him and in the love she offered, the healing would begin.

"Umu Hei Monoi," she explained as she took the last bottle from the tray. Then Adams' mind and body were caressed by a fragrance of many things. A fragrance touching every sense, awakening them, exciting them. The images in his mind were no less serene, but they were only of Eden.

As her hands stilled at last, he knew that somewhere in the delicious mélange of scents was the one Eden wore. The haunting scent he carried with him wherever he went. The scent that made him want her as he never had before.

"Eden." Turning, he found her standing by the bed. Waiting. Waiting for him. One touch of the brooch at her breasts, and the dress fell away. Like a strand of jewels the bright fabric skimmed down her body revealing the unmarred loveliness he had known before.

Her eyes told him she was as hungry for him as he was for her. Drawing her down to him, he murmured, "Umu Hei Monoi—is this how the women of Fatu Hiva soothe the moods of savage beasts?"

"Only at first." Her lips grazed his shoulder.

"And?" Adams was poised over her, his dark gaze holding hers, his body seeking the embrace of hers. "The second?"

Rising to initiate their joining and taking him deeply into herself, she couldn't answer. Their lovemaking was sweetly silent until in a heartbeat before euphoria, Eden breathed her answer in the kisses of ecstasy. "In Fatu Hiva and now Belle Terre, Umu Hei Monoi is the perfume of seduction."

"Vixen," Adams muttered into the wild disarray of her hair as quiet returned. "I think you would enchant me."

"Yes." Eden laughed softly. "Oh, yes, my love."

Six

"**A**dams?"

"Hey, buddy." Waving a hand before Adams' blank study, Jackson joined in Lincoln's prodding. "Where did you go?"

Adams looked up from a sheaf of papers to find all three of his brothers watching him curiously.

"You were a thousand miles away all of a sudden," Jefferson explained.

"Sorry." Shifting in his chair, he drew himself completely from the daydream that ambushed him at every turn. Yet, even as he forced his attention to the brothers' family conference, he knew the vision of Eden wrapped only in candlelight and the haunting fragrance of seduction would never be far from his thoughts. Never as long as he lived.

"I'm sorry, my thoughts drifted, though not for a thousand miles." Frowning in his effort to concentrate and feeling a little unsettled, he scrubbed at the furrows between his brows. "What were you saying, Lincoln?"

"What I was saying before your return from limbo is that it's hard to understand how Gus lost so much so quickly." Lincoln, the quietly pragmatic and most reasonable of the Cades, grimaced in worry. "Especially so much so quickly."

"Hell, Linc," Jackson shot back. "What was quick about it? Belle Reve has barely been solvent since the war. So how much could there be to lose?"

With a temperament as fiery as his dark-auburn hair, Jackson could always be counted on to speak bluntly. And, Adams knew, the war he spoke of was *the* war, the Civil War. The war between the Union and the Confederacy. "Given the scope of the plantation's holdings and the finances required to keep it solvent, what he lost would normally not be that much. Because he was sly about it, it didn't happen as quickly at it seems."

"What does that mean, exactly, Adams?" Jefferson asked. "Spell it out for us."

Addressing Jefferson, Adams condensed what he'd discovered in his investigation of the plantation's financial record to one single important fact. "Gus has been operating on what would be a shoestring for Belle Reve for more years than I expected. Since each of us left home, literally or figuratively, to seek our own lives, pinpoints the beginning."

"You mean, since the last of the slaves embraced emancipation, don't you?" Jackson quipped with a wry grin.

"Assuming by that, you mean when each of us was no longer here to do the work?" Adams paused as he remembered the circumstances of his leaving. Circumstances the opposite of emancipation. Then, refusing to

brood over what couldn't be changed, he agreed. "Yes.
The troubles stem from that time.

"But the worsening of conditions was gradual. So gradual someone as astute as Gus could hide it. Then, as it
became apparent Belle Reve couldn't be self-sufficient,
when the balance between income and expenses shifted
drastically, Gus went looking for new money."

"In the stock market," Jefferson supplied. Raking his
hand through his shaggy blond hair, he turned his dark-
blue gaze to the window and the land that stretched to the
horizon. Cade land, for as far as the eye could see. Valuable land, which could be sold for a fortune. But wouldn't
be as long as Caesar Augustus Cade, emperor of all he
surveyed, drew breath.

With grief and guilt marking his face, Jefferson looked
at each of his brothers. "I should have known. I was here.
Even if I wasn't living in the house, I was here daily. I
should have seen it coming. I should have stopped him."

"How?" Jackson's bark of laughter was short and de-
risive. "Since when has anybody ever been able to stop
Gus Cade when he set a course?" Eyes as blue as Jefferson's, but with strong touches of green, held the younger
man in their laserlike focus. "How the devil could any of
this be your fault, Jeffie?"

"Indeed." Lincoln joined in from his place at the end
of the table opposite Adams. "How can you possibly see
any of this as your fault? Why would you shoulder the
burden?"

"I pick up the mail for Gus. I should have suspected."

"You read his mail, Jeffie?" Adams' question was sar-
donically tongue-in-cheek, for he knew the answer.

"Good Lord, no." Jefferson managed a laugh. "I'm
not exactly into self-immolation. But I should've been

suspicious of all the mail from investment firms and law-
yers.''

"There's nothing you could've done, Jeffie." Adams
laid aside the papers that mapped the financial ruin of
Belle Reve. "There's nothing any of us could have done.
Gus is, and was, of sound mind. Belle Reve is his. So
were any funds involved."

"But who knew the old man had so much of our illustrious forefather, the first of the Cade scalawags, in him?
Who expected the gambler's legacy would be multiplied
by ten more than three centuries later?" Always the
brother to cut quickest and deepest to the core of a problem, Jackson slid his chair away from the table and paced
to the window.

"We've worn this place like a millstone around our
necks since we were kids." Abandoning the view, he spun
back to face his brothers. With the late-morning light turning his hair to dark fire, he muttered, "Maybe losing it
wouldn't be such a bad thing."

"Then if we took a vote on saving Belle Reve, you
would vote no, Jackson?" Adams watched his hotheaded
brother, who despite his temper, had the tenderest and
most generous of hearts. "Is that what you're proposing?"

"I don't know what I'm proposing, if anything, Adams."

It was strange to see the usually decisive Jackson vac-
illate. But, Adams knew, this was not an easy choice for
any of them to make. Not even for one who, like Jackson,
normally saw issues in black or white, with rarely any
shades of gray.

Adams himself saw this particular issue in black and
white, and his choice had been made. But he wouldn't
impose that choice on the others. Saving Belle Reve

would require sacrifices of time and money. If his brothers agreed to the proposal he planned to set before them, money would be no problem. Time was a different matter, and the critical issue.

"Our dilemma, as I see it, is twofold," Lincoln observed as if he were attuned to Adams' thoughts. "Money and time."

"Who has enough of either?" Jackson growled.

"We do. At least in the less-important area," Adams said quietly. "Money won't be a problem, except keeping it from Gus."

"Speak for yourself, Adams." Jackson returned from the window to take his seat again. "The trip to Ireland and the stock I brought back, coupled with the Black Arabians, tapped me out." Looking balefully from brother to brother, he shrugged. "Truthfully? I'm flat, busted broke. To raise more than a dime, I would have to sell River Trace or some stock."

Mildly, Lincoln put in his two cents. "Vets don't starve, Adams. But we don't get rich enough to bail out plantations with miles of salable land."

Jefferson's grin didn't quite touch his eyes when he spoke up. "Fishing and hunting guides don't exactly make a fortune, either." With a lift of his shoulders, he said, "My last painting sold to an art gallery for two thousand. If that can hold the wolf away from the door long enough to give us planning time, it's yours to do with as you see best, Adams."

"Thank you, Jeffie, but before we go any further with this discussion, I think I'd better explain something." Once again, Adams looked at each of the accomplished, talented men who were his brothers, admiring their different strengths, treasuring the less obvious traits they shared. "We have Cade Enterprises."

"You mean *you* have Cade Enterprises," Jackson said without a second of hesitation. "And I devoutly hope you aren't suggesting sacrificing it for Belle Reve."

"I mean *we,* Jackson." Adams stood, bracing his hands on the table. "Each of you is listed as a partner in the business. You each have twenty-four percent. I have twenty-eight."

Ignoring their stunned disbelief, Adams continued, "You haven't received any profits, because there haven't been many that didn't need to be plowed back into the company. We show millions on paper, a plant, a plane, little significant cash flow.

"But we have an offer, a very good offer. One that won't mean the sacrifice of the company."

"What the devil do you mean by this partnership stuff, Adams? Cade Enterprises is yours. We don't deserve any part of it." For once, Lincoln completely lost his calm demeanor.

"And we sure as hell can't let you sacrifice what you've worked toward for Belle Reve," Jefferson sided with Lincoln. "You've always done more than your share, but we can't let you do this. Not after the way Gus treated you."

"Amen," Jackson put in succinctly.

"You each have a share in Cade Enterprises because you deserve it. The theory behind the mechanical part that was the start of the business came from all of us here at Belle Reve. I simply refined it and applied it to a problem on the oil rigs."

"Hell, Adams! Are you asking us to believe you got the idea for a million-dollar company from working with us on farm equipment held together by little more than spit and sweat?"

Jackson, of course. Despite the serious nature of this

standoff, Adams smiled. "I'm not asking you to believe anything, Jackson. I'm telling you. The company isn't worth millions yet. On its own, it might be in a few years. It can be now, if you, as stockholders, vote to take an offer made by Jacob Helms.

"But no matter what you decide, the stock is yours. It will be yours as long as Cade Enterprises exists." Adams' face was the stern face of the older brother. "If you'll listen, I'll lay out our options. If you still insist, we can argue later."

"Tell me again why we're doing this?" Dressed only in boots, jeans, gloves and a Stetson, Lincoln swiped sweat from his face with his forearm.

"To save our father's pride?" Jefferson grunted as he hefted another fence post into place and tamped soil around it.

"What we're doing," Jackson drawled from his seat on the tractor, "is keeping the world in general, and the low country specifically, from knowing what a proud fool he's been. With the funds from the merger of *our* company, we could hire others to get this done."

The last had been accompanied by a sidelong glance at Adams, who had argued long and eloquently. Because ultimately there was no other recourse, and because the sons of Gus Cade loved the ornery bastard who was their father, Adams won.

His victory hadn't been easy or swift. Which explained why the four of them were working in twilight. To a man, they were tired and hungry, but soon it would be dark. Then they could stop, and they prayed that Gus' cook had something more substantial for supper than her usual toasted peanut-butter sandwiches. Which, Gus had glee-fully informed them, she considered her specialty, and all her duties as cook required of her. Breakfast, lunch or dinner.

Pulling his sweat-stained gloves tighter over his hands, Adams hoisted a fence post over his shoulder. "Let's finish this section and call it a day."

"I'm for that," Jackson chimed in. "As it is, my horses are going to think their throats have been cut."

"I can still help with the stock. There's nothing pressing waiting at the cabin," Jefferson offered.

"Gus said you fixed up the old fishing shack down by the marsh." Adams dropped the last post in the last hole Jackson had bored with the tractor. Jogging it into place and leveling it, he looked up, his gaze meeting Jefferson's. "I'd like to see what you've done with it sometime."

"Good Lord!" Jackson interrupted. "Where the devil did he come from? And what in blue blazes is he doing?"

"Who? Where? What?" Lincoln asked without looking up from the aged posts he was culling from a haphazard stack.

"Eden's man." Out of fatigue, Jackson spoke in shorthand. "On the porch. No," he corrected. "Now the yard. There's a fire."

Adams spun around, his gaze touching on Cullen, then moving on. The man was never far from Eden. If he'd come to Belle Reve, she had, too.

But where was she?

Adams searched the porch and the grounds, but no Eden. It made no sense until the back door opened and Gus and his chair appeared with Eden a step behind.

Hungrily Adams watched her bend over Gus, settling him in place, seeing to his comfort. Then he heard her laugh, and all the tensions and exhaustion of the day no longer mattered.

"Eden," he said softly, and didn't notice as, one by

one, his brothers turned to look at him. He didn't see the surprise that transformed into knowing and pleased smiles.

Adams thought she would come to him. He hoped she would come to him. Instead, she waved and smiled and returned to Gus. "What the devil?" he muttered under his breath. Had she come to see Gus? Why would she? he wondered.

"Lord love a duck!" Jackson exclaimed. "I smell charcoal. The big fella's cooking supper for us tycoons."

"You hope," Jefferson said. But the grin on his face said he hoped so, as well.

"There's no other logical reason for Eden's majordomo to stroll into our backyard and start a fire." Lincoln looked from one brother to the other before he asked, "Is there?"

They burst into laughter, then by silent agreement tools were put away, and with the last post left sagging the three on foot hitched a ride to the barn with Jackson on the tractor. By the time they'd seen to the Arabians and washed up the bell used to call hands from the field was clamoring, and the mouth-watering scent of cooking steaks was redolent in the evening air.

"Thank you."

"For dinner?"

"Among other things." Adams held Eden's hand loosely in his as they walked across a meadow that would be pasture again when the fence was completed. "Gus laughed tonight. Grudgingly, but he laughed. And he ate with good appetite. His nurses, when we can find them, say he usually only picks at his food."

"Cullen gets the credit there." Taking her hand from his and without missing a step, Eden slipped beneath his arm and twined her own around his waist. "He's a magician when it comes to food."

"You get no argument from me on that. But you were the one who made Gus laugh. I suspect that did him more good than the food." Adams walked in silence for a time. Her hair brushed his bare arm; her scent enveloped him in a tantalizing cloud.

Pausing on a low rise, he drew her to him, wrapping his arms about her as she leaned back against him. Twilight had come and gone. The last of the sun lay like a rim of fire over the tops of trees surrounding the manor house. The stately old building that had been the birthplace of more Cades than Adams could remember was a darker, massive profile etched against the graying of the night.

"I never thought I would be here again," he murmured into her hair. "I never thought I would see any of this again."

"I know." Moving within his embrace, she faced him. In the fall of darkness, she could see only the handsome shape of his head and shoulders. But she knew that if she could see more, there would be that well of sadness in his eyes.

Gus Cade had asked his eldest son for help. Without hesitation and seeking nothing, Adams had returned to the place he could no longer call home. And, seeking nothing, expecting nothing, he would give his father only his best. Eden fervently hoped that someday Gus would see the truth and offer his forgiveness as generously as Adams had his support.

But Eden knew Gus' forgiveness would be a long time coming. In the meantime Adams would travel a difficult road. This had been only the second day of that long, bittersweet journey. A journey destined to grow even more difficult.

"You're exhausted." She stroked his face, tracing the shape of his lips with her fingertips.

Catching her hand in his, Adams kissed her palm and turned his cheek into its comforting curve. "An ongoing condition for some time to come, I'm afraid."

"There's so much to do here. I didn't realize how much." In Eden's voice he heard shock for all she'd seen.

"None of us realized, except Jeffie. At least not until last year, when Jackson came back from Ireland and Lincoln from California. Then, just as Jeffie wouldn't tell the three of us, the three of *them* wouldn't tell me. If Gus hadn't asked for me and Jefferson hadn't called—"

Stopping his words with a touch, Eden murmured, "If Gus hadn't asked and Jefferson hadn't called, you wouldn't have come back. And I wouldn't be standing here hoping you would kiss me."

"I'm dirty, sweetheart, and I stink of horses, but if I kiss you," Adams warned softly, "it may not stop with a kiss."

His body was taut and still against hers. But the desire that rushed through him was unmistakable. "I'll take my chances," Eden whispered even as his mouth was brushing hers. "Any day."

His kiss was light and warm, but only a whisper over her lips as he groaned and wrapped her tightly in his arms. Burying his face in her hair, he drew her closer, held her more tightly, as if he could never be close enough.

"Adams?"

When she would have drawn away to look at him, to question in concern, he muttered, "Don't talk. Don't question. Don't worry about Gus or me. Just let me hold you for a minute.

"Just let me hold you, Eden."

In the cover of darkness, a worried frown crossed her face. But neither worry nor anything else on earth would have kept her from giving Adams what he wanted, what he needed.

"Yes," she said in a hushed voice as her arms circled his waist and her body curled into his. With her cheek resting over his heart, she heard the wild, ragged beat of passion. She felt the mounting, heated tension in his body. She knew the desire he valiantly fought to deny.

Adams had struggled with himself since the first time they'd made love. Eden knew, instinctively, that he fought that same battle now. Just as instinctively, she knew this night would set the course for the rest of their time together. No matter how she might want to influence him or even seduce him with heated baths and scented oils, tonight it must be his decision. Adams already had too much to bear. She would not add guilt over an affair with Eden Claibourne to the lot.

So she held him, ignoring the painful clasp of his desperate embrace, wishing she could bear even a small part of his burden. And she waited.

Time lost its meaning. Borne on a freshening breeze, the laughter of Lincoln and Jackson and Jefferson as they argued and jousted went unnoticed.

Adams was aware only of the woman in his arms. Only Eden, whose arms and lips and body offered willing surcease for all that hurt. When he lifted his face from her hair, with the lingering scent of her a part of him, he wasn't sure if he'd won his battle with the harsh man an outcast's world had made him, or lost it.

Framing her face with his hands, he lifted her mouth to his kiss and found it waiting and giving. Eden had welcomed him back into her life with gentle ease. She'd given him love and kindness such as he'd never known. Love and kindness he would keep for his own and return tenfold. But he knew he couldn't.

Eden must know that and understand.

"Eden." Stroking her lips with his fingertips, mesmerized by the satin curves, he struggled to say what he must. "I can't stay."

"I know." Her voice was hushed, resigned.

"When my purpose here is served, I'll have to go."

"Yes." Her head was thrown back. But the pale glow of the rising moon cast no light on her face, blinding him to what she needed him to see. In the veil of night, Eden only hoped he could hear in her voice that she would never try to keep him.

"I can't ask you to come with me." Adams wouldn't explain that his world was too brutal, too cold. He wouldn't tell her the callous man he had to be to survive that world didn't deserve her.

"I know," she said again as softly and tenderly as before.

"You would have me?" His fingers tangled in her hair. "Knowing the day would come when I would go and not look back?"

"I would have you, Adams, under any circumstance. For as long as I can."

"Dammit, Eden, you're not making this any easier." Whirling away, keeping his back to her, he said roughly, "Haven't you figured out that I'm trying to drive you away?"

"Only because you can't send me away?" Eden countered.

"God help me, you know I can't." Stiff fingers stabbed through his hair as if he had to punish something for his weakness. "But I should. If I were a better man, I would."

"But not because you don't want me, Adams Cade."

"Never because I don't want you." Adams' voice was harsh and tender at once.

Eden's spine straightened now that she knew the course of their lives. She could live with his conditions. In this precious time she could live with anything—even her own shortcomings as a woman—as long as he wanted her. As long as he was here, she would love him in mind and body. When he was gone, she would love him as she'd always loved him, in her heart and her soul.

She had always loved him. She would love him forever. Everyone but Adams seemed to know. Even Nicholas Claibourne had known, when he asked her to come to the Marquesas as his wife, that she loved another man. That she would always love him so completely remained one of the elements Nicholas found most attractive in his young, unquestionably faithful and compassionate American wife.

But Eden couldn't think of Nicholas now. Her mind was too full of Adams. Closing the distance he'd put between them, she laid a hand on his shoulder. He tensed but didn't face her. "I'm here, Adams. Until you can say you don't want me."

With a hoarsely muttered curse, he returned to her. His embrace was unrestrained and fierce. "I've cursed myself for not being honorable enough to send you away. I've tried, Eden. Time and again, I've tried. But, damn my selfish soul, I can't."

"I know, Adams. I know, and I'm not going away. Not as long as you want me and need me."

"How can I deserve you?"

"It isn't a question of deserving." Eden took his hand

in hers as she stepped from his embrace. "This, you and I, whatever you want to call it, has nothing at all to do with deserving or not deserving."

Adams chuckled hoarsely, and there was profound weariness in the sound. "I'd forgotten you were captain of the debating team in high school."

"Ha! You weren't in high school when I was. So how would you know?"

"I know a lot about you. Much that no one suspected I knew." His voice thickened. Dehydration, a couple of beers with dinner and full-blown exhaustion had finally taken their toll.

"Sounds like love to me," Eden teased as she slipped her arm around him to coax him back toward the house.

At some point that had escaped her notice, the younger Cades had taken their leave. Likely as wearily as Adams. With her usual foresight, Eden had asked Cullen to see to Gus before he left. In case the invisible nurses chose to remain quivering in their hiding places. Silly cowards, she recalled in disgust. Five minutes with Gus, and she had discovered that with any reasonably attractive female, his bark was worse than his bite.

In fact, the stubborn old hell-raiser could be quite charming when he wanted to be. Sometimes even when he didn't particularly want to be. Both discoveries explained his four wives for four sons.

"What did you say?" Adams stopped in the middle of the meadow, his head bent toward her.

"I said you weren't in high school with me."

"After that."

"I said it sounds like love."

"Yeah, that." Reaching for her, he drew her back to him. With his arm heavy across her shoulders, he asked, "Where were we going? Where is everyone?"

"First question—to the inn." Eden matched her pace with his. "Second question—everyone else has called it a night. Even Cullen. We're all that's left of the party."

"Did seem like a party, didn't it?" Adams looked up at the house that was dark now. "Like old times, almost."

It was always there. Even when he was numbed by too much work and worry and a morass of emotions, the hurt and sadness he thought he kept hidden still lurked and waited.

"Speak for yourself, Cade." Eden chose to tease rather than commiserate. "I thought it was better than old times. No boys with zits and roving hands."

Adams laughed aloud, his mood lifting rapidly. "Don't be so sure you escaped scot-free. In fact, I was wondering what my chances would be of enticing you into the barn." The smile he cast down at her was utterly wicked, utterly enchanting. "Have you ever made love in fresh, fragrant hay, sweet Eden?"

"Can't say that I have." With great relief, as they approached the drive, Eden saw that Cullen had taken Adams' rental car, leaving her sedan. Which would make it easier to convince Adams, ever the gentleman, to let her drive back to the inn.

"Wanna try?" Adams had gone from despair to euphoria.

Eden would like to have taken credit for the last, but she suspected it was the result of a combination of circumstances. She suspected, as well, that she would rarely see Adams so relaxed again. "It's a tempting invitation, but we wouldn't want to shock the nurses, would we?"

"A rain check?"

In the glow from the line of gas lamps that lit the drive, she caught a glimpse of a twinkle in his eyes. He was teasing her, but two could play the game. "Sure. It's a date. Making love in a loft on a mountain of hay is every girl's dream."

"Sure it is." Without an argument, Adams opened the driver's door for her, then settled himself into the passenger's seat. "You'll forgive me if I don't hold my breath?"

Eden was laughing as she steered through the tunnel of green formed by giant oaks. Wondering how long the mood could last, she drove in silence while Adams drifted into a light sleep.

"Oh, no," Eden whispered as she turned onto Fancy Row. But for a few lights, the normally quiet street would have appeared deserted, except for the chaos in front of the inn. Revolving yellow lights flashed garishly, painting the faces of the small crowd gathered on the sidewalk in eerie shades.

In response to her cry, Adams was awake and alert, his gaze clear and sharp, without fatigue. When she brought the sedan to a halt in the middle of the street, he was out of the car instantly and circling to her door.

Taking her hand, Adams crossed the walk and threaded through the crowd. He paid no attention to the whispers of the onlookers; his attention was riveted on Jericho Rivers. Looking as tired as Adams had only a short while ago, Jericho stood among a group of uniformed deputies flanked by four squad cars.

Before either Adams or Eden could speak, Jericho was addressing their unasked question. "Easy, Eden," he said, his deep voice rumbling from his massive chest. "Just a break-in. No one was hurt."

"A robbery?" Eden couldn't imagine it. A thief risked almost certain discovery, with guests and Cullen about at all hours.

"Breaking and entering, but we're not sure yet about

robbery," Jericho explained. "Cullen says nothing that belongs to the inn is missing, but we need Adams to check his personal belongings. I doubt he'll find anything missing."

"The river cottage? How? Why?" Eden looked from Jericho to Adams and intercepted a meaningful look passing between them.

"He came from the river," Adams said, rather than asked.

"We're pretty sure he did." Jericho's gaze skimmed over the gathering of onlookers. Staid and proper, even in nightclothes. "I can't see that he could go unobserved any other way."

"Even if he took something, you still won't think robbery was his motive, will you, Jericho?"

"Neither will you, when you see," the sheriff warned.

Touching her cheek, Adams bent to Eden. "Why don't you wait here, sweetheart? Jericho and I can handle this."

"No," Eden protested. "If there was an intrusion, it's my place to deal with it."

Adams didn't try to dissuade her. It hadn't taken him long to learn that Eden fought her own battles. "Then we'll go together."

Escorted by Adams and Jericho, as Eden walked to the river cottage, she remembered wondering how long Adams' good mood and happiness would last. This, she feared, was the answer.

Seven

"**O**h no!"

As Adams listened to her whispered dismay and watched helplessly, Eden wandered through the chaos. There were no tears and beyond that single, stifled cry of horror, she didn't speak.

She simply drifted through the rooms like a pale specter, her hands clasped before her as if she struggled against the urge to set things aright. But Jericho had warned that she mustn't touch, mustn't correct. What he asked of her was a visual inventory made by one most familiar with the cottage and its vintage treasures.

Cullen had done a methodical walk-through, stating that, though nothing was as it should be, neither had anything been taken. Eden understood that what the sheriff needed was her concurrence with Cullen's thoughts and his own suspicion.

Cullen was right—nothing had escaped the destruction.

Every room bore evidence of a madman's rampage. Cushions were slashed, chairs and tables were smashed or overturned. Pieces of artwork, not priceless but valuable, were shattered, slit, smashed or spattered with paint. Walls, carpet and tile were covered with obscenities in the same red paint that puddled into pools like blood.

Even the bedroom hadn't escaped the violent rampage. Not one piece of furniture remained intact. Glass from mirrors was strewn over the floor. Garbage more filthy and squalid than any Eden had ever seen had been dumped in the middle of the bed.

Garbage brought from somewhere else. All meant to violate the bed where Adams slept. Where he had made love to her.

Sickened by the desecrated memory, Eden leaned against a small space of wall that had escaped the wholesale destruction. With heavy-lidded eyes, she traced the path of a human tornado.

No, she corrected herself. Not a tornado, human or inhuman. This was too methodical. Too purposeful. Too intently malevolent. And very carefully planned.

She'd walked through the river cottage like a zombie. Now she became aware of an incongruous fragrance. A gentle, seductive fragrance, obscene in this circumstance.

Eden raised her head and her gaze sought Adams. Adams who hadn't touched her and hadn't spoken, but had never been more than a touch or a word away, if she needed either. If she needed him. When their eyes met now, she knew he recognized the fragrance of spilled Umu Hei Monoi mingling with the stench of garbage. She knew the memories it stirred, the regret he felt as deeply as she.

"Who?" she murmured. "Why?"

"We don't know, Eden. Not for sure." Jericho moved from the bedroom doorway to stand by her side.

Jericho, as big as a bear and twice as tough, twice as grim. Only Cullen was bigger, tougher, grimmer. Eden knew both would protect her and all that was hers with their lives. Yet it was the smaller, leaner man, who watched her with his heart in his eyes, for whom she longed.

"You don't know, but you have an idea, don't you?" If she hadn't known Jericho well enough to read the truth in his manner, she would have guessed from the look that had passed between the sheriff and Adams on the walk.

"An idea is all we have. We'll check it out thoroughly." Jericho's tone was apologetic. "But an idea and proof are two different matters. To be honest, I don't expect to find any proof.

"This…" A gesture encompassed the room and the cottage. "This may look like mindless destruction, but there was nothing mindless about it. Insane, maybe, but not mindless. I would stake my reputation on my conviction that whoever did this left nothing behind. No clues, no fingerprints, no telltale reminders to taunt us. Nothing."

"You mean Junior Rabb, don't you?" Eden's shadowed gaze met Adams' first, before moving to Jericho. "You were afraid of something like this. That's why you came to warn Adams the night his brothers were at the inn. You expected it."

Jericho's face grew grimmer. "I expected some sort of retaliation, yes. But nothing like this. I didn't anticipate anything so soon, or that you would be dragged into it."

"Jericho." As Adams moved to take Eden's arm, he looked up at the taller man. "Eden's seen enough. Surely we can continue this conversation in more pleasant surroundings.''

"You're right," Jericho conceded. "We can and we should.''

"I assume you have a few more details and procedures to attend to here." Barely waiting for Jericho's nod of assent, Adams continued, "While you're finishing up, I'd like to take Eden to the inn. When she's comfortable and you're ready, I'll come back to check through my personal things.''

Casting a last look at the mayhem, for which he vowed penance if not retribution, Adams scowled in angry disgust. "I agree with Jericho. This was malicious destruction, sending a warning.''

With Jericho's accord, escorted by the broodingly silent Cullen who hovered like an avenging angel with no focus for his vengeance, Adams walked with Eden to the inn. In the library, Cullen excused himself with a bow and a fiercely protective look, then left them. But, Adams knew beyond any doubt, the islander wouldn't go far from Eden or for very long.

"I'm sorry, Eden," Adams said dejectedly when they were alone and she had dropped to the sofa in shock and exhaustion. "I'm sorry I did this to you.''

"*You're* sorry?" Eden's eyes were huge. Strain from the ordeal lay beneath them like bruises. "I won't let you shoulder the blame for what happened here tonight. It wasn't your fault.''

"But I was the target." Adams had risen from his chair to pace the room. Like a claustrophobic jungle cat, he moved with lethal grace from window to door and corner to corner. "There's no denying it. If I hadn't been the current occupant of the river cottage, it would still be as pristine as the day I arrived.''

"It will be again." Eden abandoned argument in favor of optimism. "As soon as Jericho completes his investigation, we can call in the cleaning service, the upholsterers and the painters. The cottage will be as good as new."

"Will it?" Adams halted in his pacing to look at her. "What about the paintings? The pottery? Have you forgotten the splintered decoys? They can't be replaced or repaired."

"They were insured."

"Right." Bitterness turned his voice harsh. "If I remember my history correctly, this house has been in your family for years. No," Adams corrected, "for centuries. Some of the treasures you lost tonight were part of your family legacy."

Crossing to her, putting a finger beneath her chin, he lifted her face for his scrutiny. "When I was growing up, I heard Gus talk about the decoys—how old they were, how rare, how valuable. I know they were part of your father's collection, and his favorites. Gus didn't admire many people, but Ted Roberts, collector and hunter extraordinaire, was an exception."

A strange expression, a mix of surprise and amazement, flitted over Adams' face. "I'd forgotten until this minute that the only time I ever saw Gus shed a tear was when he heard your mother and dad were lost on a hunting expedition near the Amazon."

For the second time in Eden's presence, Adams had recalled a forgotten facet of Gus' personality. A recollection that made the unbending martinet more human. "If Gus cared that much, then Ted Roberts must have been quite a man."

"He lived to hunt," Eden said. "My mother lived for him. So much so that she left me with my grandparents regularly to go with him on his hunts. I was two when they were lost in a boating accident on the Amazon. I don't remember them, Adams.'' Holding his gaze, refusing to be distracted, she added softly, ''Yes, the decoys were my father's and, yes, they're irreplaceable. I never wanted to lose them, but I won't die for the lack of them.''

She almost added, as she might for the lack of Adams. But, just this evening, she'd made her bargain with him and with herself. She would let him go on his own terms, when he must. But not yet. Not because of the vengeful hatred of Junior Rabb.

''We'll rebuild and repair. I've done it before. You were right, River Walk has been in my family forever. One of my distant grandfathers had it built for his mistress. After that the house had a checkered past. Some of it pleasant, some not. Finally it became the family repository. A tattered remnant of lost affluence, reduced to a warehouse for family junk. And, finally, my parents' and grandparents' treasures.''

''You say 'junk' and 'remnant,' Eden. But when you returned to Belle Terre to reclaim the house, you could refurbish with the authentic, irreplaceable family heirlooms that were waiting for you. All of which, along with your own artistry, contribute to the unique charm of River Walk and the cottage,'' Adams finished for her, refusing to allow her to disparage all she'd accomplished and all she'd lost. ''An invaluable part has been taken from you and from River Walk in an act of malicious vandalism. Because of me.''

Tilting her cheek into his palm, Eden covered his hand with hers. ''The decoys can be repaired. They were before, when my father found them and restored them. The paintings, the sculptures were copies and can be replaced. In no time, the river cottage will look as if nothing ever happened. You'll see.''

"No, Eden." Taking his hand from her clasp, giving himself space to say what he must, Adams walked away. Not to the window, not to the view of the cottage. He needed no reminder that he'd brought this down on her because of who he was, perhaps, because of what he'd become. "I can't stay here. It was a mistake to choose River Walk in the first place."

Eden had grown pale. "If you leave Belle Terre, will you leave your brothers, as well? Must they save Belle Reve alone?"

Adams turned away from Eden's distress. "I should leave, go back where I belong. If I had half a functioning brain, I would say to hell with Belle Reve, Belle Terre and Junior Rabb. But I gave my word to Gus. And I owe it to my brothers to stay."

"Then you're only leaving River Walk and Belle Terre."

"As soon as Jericho gives me the okay."

"Why, Adams? I knew you would leave someday." Because she didn't want him to see her despair, Eden looked down at her hands as they lay twined and rigid in her lap. "Why now?"

"Have you not been listening? Dammit, can't you see that I caused this? How many times do I have to say it?" As her head lifted and her stricken look met his, Adams couldn't continue his tirade. He couldn't bear not touching her, not comforting her.

In swift strides he crossed to her, taking her in his arms as he sat by her. "I'm sorry." Cradling her head against his shoulder, he kissed her hair, her cheeks, her eyes. "I'm not angry with you. How could I be?"

Moving her away from him only the little needed to look at her, he traced the line of her cheek. "I'm not leaving because I want to. I *have* to. If this was Junior

Rabb tonight, he's shown how much he hates me and how dangerous his hatred can be.

"If he can't destroy me, he'll destroy something of mine. Where I live, what I love, anything." Drawing her back into his arms, resting his cheek on her gleaming hair, he spoke softly. "If he suspected we were ever lovers, he would come after you. I can't let than happen, Eden. If he hurt you…"

"He won't, Adams." Eden pulled away. Her eyes were blazing with anger. "He's too much the coward. He saves his wrath for inanimate objects. Not people who can see how little he is."

"Maybe," Adams agreed quietly. "But we can't take that chance. *I* can't take that chance."

With a shake of her head, Eden stared at him, not comprehending the dire promise he made.

"Don't you see, sweetheart?" Framing her face between thumb and forefinger, with her chin nestled in the juncture, he lifted her face again, capturing her gaze. Keeping it. "I didn't kill him thirteen years ago. But if he hurt you, or even tried…this time I would."

"So, to protect me you would leave and break off all contact." She kept her voice calm and level. What he was proposing was exactly what she should've expected of Adams Cade, ever her champion. Ever her protector. Not because he feared the consequences of his actions, but because he feared for her.

"There's no other option, Eden. None."

Because he felt so strongly, to entice her into agreement he tried to make it seem as if he were protecting himself from what he might do. Eden would never be fooled by such an absurd thought. But for Adams, because he needed her compliance, however achieved, she would yield to his judgment.

Caught in his mesmerizing gaze, with a small tilting of her head, Eden expressed her silent, reluctant agreement.

"Then you understand?" Adams must have her say the words. He had to know she understood the danger and that, when he was gone from her, she would be cautious.

"Yes, Adams," Eden repeated dutifully, "I understand."

"Thank you." He would have kissed her then. With the devil or Junior Rabb looking on, he would have kissed her. But the last opportunity was snatched from him.

"Adams." Jericho stood in the doorway with Cullen hovering behind him. "We're ready for you at the cottage."

"I'll be there shortly, Jericho."

"You need a minute to say your goodbyes." The sheriff smiled his permission, though he knew it was ridiculous. Adams would say and do what he intended with or without permission. "I'll wait in the kitchen."

When Jericho had gone and Cullen had disappeared, Adams gathered her hands in both of his. Lifting them to his mouth, with his lips he stroked her knuckles and the delicate tracery of veins that shone pale blue beneath the sun-warmed color of her skin. "Take care," he said softly, "never be alone in public places. Never forget our caution may be pitifully late. Junior might know what we've been to each other. I don't know how, but he might.

"If he has any idea, he'll understand that hurting you would be more intolerable than anything he could do to me." Adams voice took on a desperate note. "Jericho will assign a deputy to watch over you. But count on yourself. Listen to your own instincts. Never let down your guard. Never, sweetheart."

Releasing her as she stared wordlessly at him, Adams

stood. Towering over her, he touched her cheek one last time and left her without a backward look.

Numb and incapable of moving, Eden heard the murmur of voices in the hall. Cullen had lurked just beyond the door. Not eavesdropping—the massive islander would never deliberately eavesdrop. But he would protect her as Adams would. As Adams had.

Their voices were low but clear, as Eden heard Adams charge Cullen with her care. "Keep her safe, Cullen."

"I will," the normally reticent islander replied.

"If Junior Rabb should come, if he should hurt her..."

"I will kill him." Cullen's reply was his solemn vow.

"I know. I've always known." After a pause Adams spoke again. "Thank you for all you've done for her."

"Doing for Mistress Eden is one of life's pleasures, Mr. Adams. I have no need for gratitude."

There was more Eden didn't understand, and the report of flesh against flesh. A familiar sound recalling the salute of boys and young men. Cullen had just been inducted into the brotherhood of the Cades. Stranger things could happen, but nothing kinder.

A kindness that eased her own despair as she listened to the cadence of retreating footsteps. Adams footsteps.

"Mr. Adams." The islander's call halted his departure.

"Just Adams, Cullen."

"Yes, a good name. I will miss you, Adams Cade. We will all miss you. When this is resolved, you will come back."

"Wishful words, for all of us. But no, I won't be back."

Eden heard footsteps once again, and the quiet closing of a door. Her head was down, her eyes hot and burning, when she felt a touch at her shoulder.

"He's wrong," Cullen said in his little-used voice. "He will be back. I promise."

"The officer in charge isn't at her desk at the moment, but she asked that I escort you to Sheriff Rivers' office." The baby-faced deputy, who looked barely old enough to be trusted with a razor, circled the absent officer's desk. "Right this way, sir."

As Adams followed the young man's lead, a memory surfaced. His escort was Court Hamilton, who had been twelve, a friend of Jefferson's and a rising baseball star, when Adams left the low country. He would be twenty-five now, a year younger than Jefferson. Yet he looked much younger.

Time and circumstances and coping with Gus hadn't robbed Jefferson of his startling, golden-boy good looks. Yet they had stamped him with a visage of maturity beyond his years.

With Lincoln and Jackson, and Jefferson, as well, the hardships of their lives were readily apparent. In the lines and heavy-shouldered musculature of their bodies. In the weathered tone of their skin. All of which spoke of grueling physical labor—in sun, or rain, or heat, and in the cold.

The level, shrewd and sometimes penetrating gaze of each spoke of phenomenal discipline and determination. But of all the brothers, including Adams, only Jefferson bore the haunted look.

A truth that Court Hamilton, with his lingering youth and unmarked face, brought home as nothing ever had. Of course, Adams had known Jefferson suffered when his eldest brother was sentenced to years in prison. Until this vivid comparison, he'd never understood the depth or the toll of that suffering.

"Here you are, sir."

Adams looked into bright, clear eyes, but it was Jefferson's he saw. Beautiful eyes, as darkly blue as the evening sky. Eyes with the truth of his emotions carefully shielded.

The incident with Junior Rabb had changed all their lives. Altered how they felt about themselves. Adams wondered now if prison hadn't been easier than what Jefferson had been left to face, too young and alone.

"Sir?"

Adams heard the confusion in Officer Hamilton's voice and shook off the pall of distraction. "I beg your pardon?"

"Sheriff Rivers will see you now."

Adams was half expecting the formal young man to salute him. Instead, he threw open the door to Jericho's office and motioned Adams inside.

"Adams." Looking every inch the astute and intuitive law-enforcement officer he was, Jericho laid down a yellowing folder and stood to offer his hand. "You're prompt. Thank you for that."

Ignoring the folder, Adams chuckled. "Old habits die hard, don't they? I wonder if any of the courtesies Lady Mary drilled into her pupils were ever forgotten."

"Not likely." Jericho chortled. "It would mean our lives, even today, if she thought we did."

"She's still alive?" Adam's brows lifted in surprise.

"Certainly, and not a bit shy about cracking the knuckles of her former pupils caught in transgressions." Jericho sobered. "She would love to see you. The Cades were her favorites, in turn. Especially Jefferson. Maybe she recognized he was the more sensitive of the rambunctious musketeers."

"Rambunctious?" Adams took the seat indicated. "I

suppose we were, without the influence of a mother, or mothers, as the case was." Mention of the maiden lady who lived alone in a crumbling city home of her forefathers brought back memories. "In some things Gus aspired for finer things for his sons.

"When we were of the proper age, twice a week, rain or shine, he spiffed us up, slicked back our hair and marched us into Lady Mary's house for instruction in the art of being gentlemen. Twice a week for two years, she drilled habits into us that would last a lifetime." Adams chuckled again. "I still have trouble with ladies who object to doors being opened for them. I feel like Lady Mary is looking over my shoulder expecting that I insist a lady must act as she thought ladies should."

"I was half-grown before I realized her name was Mary Alston, and teaching unruly children manners and ballroom dancing was her way of supplementing a very small income." As Jericho spoke, he riffled the pages of the report he'd abandoned.

"I hated her classes and called them sissy stuff then. But if I had children and lived in Belle Terre, there's nothing I would like better than to expose them to Lady Mary's teachings."

"But you won't be." Jericho shot a considering look at Adams. "You won't be staying or living in Belle Terre."

Adams knew then the time of reminiscing had ended. "Once I've finished with what I came to do, I'll be leaving. It's best for everyone that I go."

"I doubt Eden or your brothers would agree with that." Pages riffled again, but Jericho didn't say any more.

"It's because of Eden and my brothers that I have to leave. I think you know that as well as I do, Jericho."

"Because of Junior Rabb and the incident last night at

the river cottage? For which, by the way, Mr. Rabb offered an airtight alibi." A hint of frustration slipped beyond Jericho's iron control and colored his voice in the last words of his comment.

"Can you think of a better reason?" Adams countered.

"Actually I can't think of any reason at all." Leaving his desk, Jericho crossed to the window. For a time he was silent, deep in his thoughts.

Adams was familiar with the tactic of silence. One that often spurred the uninitiated to fill the void with nervous conversation and unintentional revelations. As a veteran practitioner of the strategy, he kept his own silence and bided his time.

Jericho turned from the window, a conceding, humorless smile on his craggy face. "It never made sense, you know."

Adams sat stolidly, keeping his own silence.

"We were friends, Adams. I knew you as well as I knew myself. Sometimes better. You were always slow to anger but quick to forgive. I can't remember how many times I watched you face down a troublemaker or a bully with only that lazy, cocksure grin. But when you fought, it was the last resort. You never went looking for trouble in your life. Dammit, Adams!" Pausing, Jericho scraped a palm across his chin and turned a grim look to the man who had been his trusted childhood friend. "You might never run from trouble, but you never in your life went looking for it."

"Obviously I did, in Rabb Town, thirteen years ago."

"No." Jericho returned to his desk, his fists braced on the folder. "It goes too much against the grain. There's something you aren't telling me. The same thing you didn't tell the man who was sheriff of Belle Terre then."

Snatching up the folder, Jericho held it toward Adams.

"I've gone over this more times than I can remember, searching for something that will explain what you were supposed to have done. Like tigers, Cades don't change stripes, Adams."

"Tsk, tsk, Jericho. Don't tell me computerization hasn't swept through the police department of Belle Terre." Adams shook his head in mock surprise. "Surely our illustrious city isn't so backward that you had to go digging into files that should be marked ancient history, over and done with."

Jericho wouldn't be distracted. "Oh, it's been cannibalized by our computer system. Never doubt that. But I wanted the original. I wanted to hold these particular papers in my hand. I keep thinking there's something somebody missed and maybe it's here. Missed even by the blasted computers."

"Holding a yellowing sheaf of papers is going to tell you something the same report reprinted on crisp new paper won't?" Adams' laugh was friendly mockery. "Have you taken up divining? Is that what this is all about? Are you *reading* old papers like the elderly Gypsy who lived down near the wharf read palms and tea leaves and tarot cards for us when we were kids?"

"Funny one, Cade," Jericho drawled as he had in the past when he thought Adams was hustling him. "Just to let you know, as far as I'm concerned, nothing this full of holes is ever over and done with. It shouldn't have been then. It isn't now."

"Leave it, Jericho." Adams' voice took on a harsh note. "You've enough to do without dragging out old files. I repeat, it's ancient history."

"Maybe it was." Jericho tossed the file onto his desk, ignoring the stained pages that spilled from it. "It isn't anymore, thanks to Junior Rabb."

"We're back to the incident at the cottage." Adams sighed heavily. A muscle quivered in his cheek as his teeth closed in a hard clench.

"Doesn't everything come full circle, Adams?" Jericho asked quietly. "And in this, the end of the circle is you, and the answers only you can give me."

"I have no answers for you, Jericho. None I didn't give at the time."

It was Jericho's moment to sigh. His turn to clench his jaw. "All right," he said suddenly, flexing massive shoulders as if he'd been too tense for too long. "We'll leave it at that."

"For now," Adams interpreted.

"For now," Jericho agreed.

"Then if this little talk is finished..."

Adams had begun to rise when Jericho spoke again. "There are a couple more things."

"Okay." Adams dropped back into his seat, his elbows resting on the arms of the chair, his fingers steepled before his face. "Let's hear it."

"First, I've assigned a deputy to watch over Eden. Though with Cullen hovering like a tiger, anyone I send is superfluous.

"I would assign one to you—"

"No!" Adams shot back.

"—but I know you wouldn't tolerate it," Jericho finished as if the interruption had never happened. "In any case, the day you can't best Junior Rabb—if he ever decided to come at you face-to-face—is the day I might believe this."

Adams watched as the sheriff's long fingers scattered the papers of the old report even more. "Put it away, Jericho," he said softly. "There's nothing you can learn from it."

Jericho's narrowed gaze said that, to his frustration, he knew that better than anyone. "You've moved out of the cottage."

"I thought it best. For Eden's sake."

"Bunking with Jackson in that tumbledown farmhouse while his horses sleep in state-of-the-art barns? Must be interesting."

It came as no surprise that Jericho knew where he was staying. "Just one barn so far. He ran out of money before he could finish up at River Trace or Belle Reve."

"He expects to run horses at both places?"

"Is would be better to say he's going to try." Rising from his chair again, Adams said, "Now, if that's all …"

Jericho stood, as well, offering his hand. "I'm not your enemy, Adams. I could never be anything but your friend."

"I know." Ignoring the sheriff's big hand, Adams clasped his forearm in the salute of their youth. "I've always known that, Jericho. I only wish you could understand why circumstances have to be as they are."

"Maybe someday I will."

"Maybe not," Adams returned as he stepped back, and with the slow infectious grin Jericho remembered, he opened the door and left.

Eight

"Look at him."

Jackson put aside the bridle he had mended and took up another as he joined Adams at the barn door. "Yeah," he said softly as he looked out over the training paddock. "Look at him."

"I'd forgotten how amazing he is on a horse." Another bridle dangled over Adams' arm as he watched Jefferson put a horse through its paces. "If I didn't know better, I would swear that horse and Jeffie read each other's minds."

"Yeah." Jackson tipped back the brim of his hat. "I couldn't have made a go of this if it weren't for Jeffie. Since I brought the Irish stock to River Trace and moved the Arabians to Belle Reve, he's worked night and day with me. Lincoln, too, when he could. But even before Dad's stroke, Jeffie started with the Arabians by dawn every day, did what the old man wanted done there.

"Then he would disappear for most of the afternoon. But always without fail, before sundown, he was back to check on Dad and Belle Reve, then he came to River Trace."

"To work with the horses," Adams murmured, his gaze still on the youngest Cade.

"Better than anybody I've ever seen." A bridle jingled as Jackson tossed it onto a peg by the door. "His fishing and hunting guide service is seasonal, but it could be amazingly profitable."

"*Could* be," Adams said, emphasizing the point, "if he spent the time with it." His bridle joined Jackson's. Once, the successful toss would have drawn a grin, but neither man felt like smiling as they pondered the gentlest of the brothers who worked his magic with a temperamental stallion. "If there was any time left over for it after all the responsibility he's shouldered."

"Yeah," Jackson said. "He's been like this since, well, for a long time."

"Since I left Belle Reve," Adams finished more precisely.

Jackson nodded once, abruptly. "He quit being a kid the day the judge handed down your sentence. It was as if he decided he had to fill your shoes and his, too. He's worked nonstop day and night, like a man driven. He wouldn't have finished high school or gone to college if Gus hadn't raised so much hell about it."

Adams laughed then. A dry, humorless sound, ending almost before it began. "Other than Belle Terre and work, only two things ever mattered to Gus."

"That we learn all Lady Mary could teach us about being gentlemen and that we get an education. How we managed to pay for the last was our problem, but we were to do it." Jackson sighed, remembering. "For such a sweet person, our Lady Mary could be as tough as the old man. She cracked my shin so many times it's a wonder her cane didn't wear out.''

"But she never hurt you.''

"Nah.'' Jackson stepped from the barn into the glow of sunset. "But she didn't quite make a gentleman of me, either.''

Only another man would agree, never the ladies, Adams thought. His attention returned to Jefferson. "He works at his own businesses just enough to keep body and soul together. The rest of himself he gives to the family.''

"Not even any social life. Though not for lack of trying on the ladies' part. They practically swoon at his feet. If Jeffie noticed, he might pick them up and dust them off, then devastate them with a smile before he walked away.'' Jackson's lips quirked in a puzzled frown. "The kid's got it all—looks, personality, an uncanny ability to capture real life on canvas.''

"But like his guide service, he only does it enough to make ends meet.'' Adams had lived at River Trace for a month, going every day at dawn to Belle Reve. There he worked nonstop until nearly evening. Then it was back to River Trace for more work with the horses. Jackson and Jefferson were with him every step of the way. Every minute of the day. "When does he find time to paint?''

"Beats me.'' Jackson stepped farther into the training paddock to signal for Jefferson to come in. Over his shoulder, to Adams he said, "But find it he does. You should see the portrait he painted of Robbie…I mean, Eden, for her birthday.

"Jeffie,'' Jackson said. "Finish up and call it a day. The horse has had enough, even if you haven't.''

"A horse will work its heart out for him,'' Adams commented as Jefferson guided the horse through the last exercises. The image of a portrait of Eden filled his thoughts. How did Jeffie portray her? What special qualities did he capture on canvas?

Adams would give his soul for a glimpse. But he couldn't and he wouldn't, he knew, as he dragged his thoughts back to his brother. "You know as well as I do, Jackson, that he senses when the horse has had enough. It's Jeffie you're calling in."

"He has the touch. More than any of us." Jackson paused as a sedan made the last curve in the long drive leading to River Trace. "Looks like we have company."

"Eden's car." There was a leap of concern in Adams' voice as a frown gathered on his rugged features. "She shouldn't be here. It's too dangerous."

"She isn't, Adams." Drawing his hat down a notch to shade his eyes, Jackson squinted at the car. "Unless I'm going blind from too much work, that's Cullen at the wheel, with the pretty little maid, what's-her-name, in the passenger seat."

"You're right." Adams was suddenly alarmed. Fear clogged his throat as he moved quickly from the barn and was waiting in the drive by the time Cullen brought the sedan to a halt. Wrenching open the driver's door, Adams asked in a low, desperate tone, "What's wrong, Cullen? Why are you here? Is Eden hurt? Is—"

"Mistress is fine," Cullen interrupted, "given the circumstances. From the looks of this, maybe better than you."

Climbing from the car, the big man closed the door before facing Adams. "It's hard, isn't it?" he said kindly, yet surely. "Especially when you've both cared so much for so long."

The islander had never presumed to make personal remarks before. But after observing Cullen at his work in his silently effective way and knowing how attuned he was to all things regarding Eden, Adams wasn't surprised he'd perceived so much.

"It's hard," Adams admitted. "But I've faced hardship before. I can again."

"So has Mistress, but why must she now?" Cullen asked almost casually. "What purpose does it serve?"

"You know why, Cullen. You know what purpose." Adams looked away, his gaze finding, but not focusing on, Merrie as she leaned against the paddock fence. "The river-cottage vandalism was directed at me. Maybe we can't prove it, but we don't have to have proof to know. I can't risk bringing any more trouble down on her."

"And if she was more than willing to take the risk?" When Adams didn't respond, Cullen continued, "This Junior Rabb person could have gotten to her before, if he'd wanted. But he didn't and he won't. He's cowardly, and unless he's insane, he won't dare touch her."

"If she's in the way when he tries for me?" Adams settled a bleak look on the unlined face of the islander. "What then?"

"If he ever comes after you, if he's sane, it will be from behind, when you're alone. That's the coward's way, Adams."

"I can't risk it, Cullen." Adams shook his head slowly. "I'd rather give her up than lose her forever.

"I can't have her. It was never in the cards. But knowing she's somewhere in the world, making it a better and splendid place, is enough." When Cullen would have argued, Adams silenced him with a lift of his hand. "Subject closed. Is that all that brought you out here? Or is there more?"

After speaking with Merrie, Jackson had hung back barely within hearing of the deadly serious conversation.

Stepping forward, he explained, "Cullen's brought us help. It seems Eden's little Merrie is from Argentina, and she's an expert horsewoman."

"Indeed," Cullen confirmed. "Merrie is more than expert with horses. She loves them to distraction. Which is why her mother, who was a friend of Mistress Eden's roommate in college, asked her to take the child in. Vincente Alexandre is fearful their daughter will grow up to be a gaucho, rather than a lady. Who better to teach her to be a gentlewoman than an old friend of an old friend? Especially if that teacher is Mistress Eden?"

Adams recognized the name of one of the wealthiest and most influential men in Argentina. "Mr. and Mrs. Alexandre sent their daughter to study in Belle Terre and to work as a maid while she learns to be a lady?" Laughing softly, he added, "You must admit, Cullen, it sounds more than a little farfetched."

"Not when you're the daughter of Vincente Alexandre. He believes all people should understand working for one's opportunities. His daughter, especially, is no exception. It was only on the contingency that she make herself useful to Mistress Eden that he agreed to let her come to America and Belle Terre."

Cullen was becoming positively chatty. Which led Adams to be suspicious. "So, Merrie's sent from Argentina to keep her away from horses and suddenly it's all right that she comes to River Trace to work with Jackson's herd?"

"The situation has been cleared with her family. They have no objection to her having contact with horses, as long as she not eat and sleep with the horses and the gauchos as she was prone to do in Argentina."

Though Jackson knew Cullen meant it in a totally different context, the idea of an exuberant innocent like Merrie sleeping in the carnal sense with anyone made him smile.

"If she truly knows her stuff, Merrie can help." Jackson focused his attention on the girl as she concentrated on the stallion performing perfectly under Jefferson's command. "I give you and Eden, and Mr. and Mrs. Alexandre, my personal guarantee that she won't sleep with horses or gauchos. In fact, I don't think the problem will ever come up. I noticed at the inn when Adams arrived that, beyond a look of appreciation, the little lady from Argentina is immune even to Jeffie. That's gotta be a first."

"Then you won't mind if she comes out most evenings to work, Mr. Jackson?"

"It's Jackson, Cullen, just plain Jackson." With a grin Jackson lifted his hat to scrub a hand over his short auburn hair. "If she proves to be as good as you say, she's welcome anytime. So long as it doesn't interfere with school or her schedule at the inn."

"That won't be a problem. Merrie's young, but she's quite intelligent. When it comes to horses, I think you'll find her earnestly serious," Cullen assured him. "So if that's settled, we should be going. Mistress Eden will be expecting us. But before we go, there is one more thing." The islander reached inside his jacket and drew out a stack of vellum envelopes. "These."

Curious, Adams took the envelope addressed to him. The handwriting wasn't the one he expected. Eden had written him frequently, at first, when he was in prison. After months of stony silence from him, she'd finally stopped. He'd read those letters over and over, devouring them, memorizing them. Until, fearful they would become too tattered to read again in troubled times, he put them away. Leaving the rest to memory.

Adams still had those sanity-preserving letters. He didn't look at them or read them anymore. But he would know Eden's hand anywhere, anytime. Even on his deathbed.

"Ah, the invitation," Jackson said as he took his. "We've been so busy I didn't realize it was that time."

"Invitation? Time?" As the renegade of the Cade family—and, perhaps of the entire land—Adams wouldn't have expected to be invited anywhere, anytime, by anyone.

"It's for Mistress' birthday party." Cullen offered Adams the invitations addressed, respectively, to Jefferson and Lincoln. "It's always quite a lovely party. Guests who've stayed with us regularly come from all over the country and sometimes the world to be here for this night."

"Cullen, I can't—"

The islander stopped Adams protest with a hand raised palm out. "Don't refuse yet. Give it a few days. Consider it. Weigh her disappointment against the minute chance that Junior Rabb would be so bold as to commit an act of violence in the presence of so many influential and important people."

When Adams still would have protested, Cullen bowed a goodbye and turned his back on him. Striding to the fence, where Merrie stood mesmerized by Jackson's fabulous horse, he effectively negated any chance of argument.

"Eden gives herself a birthday party?" Adams grimaced. The idea was totally out of character. "What's worse, she sends her custodian to insure that I come? No. That makes no sense."

"Maybe because you have it all wrong, brother Adams."

Adams shot Jackson a skeptical look. "You heard him, same as I did. Eden's having a party and we're expected to appear."

"Eden isn't having a party." Jackson enunciated each word carefully, as if his brother was missing a screw, or deaf, or both. "You know as well as I that this is the last thing she would ever do. The lady has too much class for anything so self-serving. And—" he leaned hard on the word, nailing down attention already riveted on him "—you should know, she wouldn't demand that anyone be present."

"No," Adams agreed. "Especially not me."

Jackson's blue-green gaze regarded him steadily. "What you mean is, especially not someone who walked out on her and didn't look back a second time."

"I didn't walk out."

"Didn't you? Then tell me, Adams, what do you call waltzing back into her life, stirring up old feelings, then poof!" Jackson flipped his fingers against his thumb in a dramatic gesture. "Just like that, you're gone."

"It isn't like that," Adams protested. "There are circumstances you don't understand. Circumstances…"

In a hand-out gesture mimicking Cullen, Jackson stopped the explanation. "Tell it to the one who needs to understand. Tell it to Eden at her birthday party. That should make her day."

"Dammit, Jackson, I won't be seeing Eden. I won't be making a command performance."

"Good." Jackson crossed his arms over his chest, a gesture that had survived from childhood, signaling he'd chosen his side and dug in. Nothing would, or could, sway him now. No argument, no explanation. Not even, if this were a tavern and Adams not his brother, would a brawl. "While you're explaining, big brother, take a minute to include how bad, bad Junior Rabb will keep you from attending the birthday party her employees and guests give her each year.''

"Employees and guests." Adams felt like an idiot. "I should have known. You're right, throwing a party for herself is the last thing Eden would do."

"Maybe you would've known, if you weren't trying so hard *not* to see the truth." On that sage observation, Jackson spun on his boot heel and stalked away to join Cullen and Merrie by the paddock.

Adams glared at his brother's back, wondering why the world and his family had ganged up on him over an issue as straightforward as protecting Eden Claibourne.

"I won't go. Commanded presence or not." Even to himself, he sounded like a broken record. But it didn't keep him from adding, "Special night for Eden or not, I can't go."

Leaving the drive, he returned to the barn to begin again the tedious chores he'd set for himself. The sedan was gone when a weary Lincoln slid onto the bench beside him.

"Tough day?"

"You could say so." Lincoln leaned back against the wall, his eyes closed and a smile on his face. "If you call saving a prize mare and her twin colts hard, that is."

"Troubled delivery, huh?" Adams laid a frayed rope aside.

"Touch and go, and long. The mare gave out."

"But you got 'em."

"Yeah."

Adams clapped Lincoln on the shoulder. "Congratulations. You sound like a proud papa."

"I feel like a proud papa."

"By the way, Cullen brought an invitation by for you." Adams tried to keep his voice casual.

Without opening his eyes, Lincoln said, "Ah, this will be an invitation to Eden's birthday party."

"How did you know?"

"It's July, Adams." Lincoln lifted a shoulder as if that statement alone were enough to explain. But he didn't leave it there. "In two weeks it will be August. Eden's birthday is the first of August, and her staff throws a bash in her honor on that day. They have for years. God willing, they will for many more."

Still leaning against the wall, Lincoln opened one eye and turned his head just enough to study Adams. "You *are* going, aren't you? I know you've been acting like a jackass, but surely you won't disappoint the lady on her special day."

Clapping his hands on his knees, Adams asked in disgust, "What is this—some sort of conspiracy? Are you all as obtuse as you've always seemed? Can't you see? Don't you know?"

"What I see—" Lincoln still regarded him with one eye as he stemmed the flow "—is two people who love each other like crazy. Always have. Always will. Except one is too stubborn to just give in to it and be grateful."

"There's one small detail you all keep overlooking."

"Junior Rabb," Lincoln supplied. "I would say a lot of sound and fury, signifying nothing. Instead, I'll tell it like it is. A cowardly windbag who wages war on smaller people and inanimate objects. And then, only in secret."

"You don't think he will hurt Eden?"

"Not if he's sane." Rolling his head back to a more comfortable position, Lincoln's grin turned grim. "Too many of us badasses would skin him alive. Surely you know that, Adams. If you don't, you should. Junior sure as hell does.''

''I can't take the chance.'' Adams knew how every male within her circle felt about Eden. But it changed nothing.

''Suit yourself.'' Folding his hands over his middle, Lincoln gave himself up to weariness. He was so still Adams thought he slept. When he spoke, his deep voice was startling. ''We need to consider bearding the lion.''

''By that I assume you mean Gus,'' Adams drawled.

''Who else?'' Lincoln was suddenly totally alert. ''I was down by the walnut grove today. The trees should never have survived, but we have a good stand of timber there. Could run into millions when the time's right. With the right choices.''

''Such as?'' Adams listened when Lincoln spoke of timber. The second Cade son had earned a degree in forestry before veterinary medicine. Because he loved trees almost as much as animals, he was a volunteer firefighter. A smoke jumper.

''The last two years were dry. This year was drier. Next year is predicted to be the driest yet. The grove's a tinderbox waiting for a match.'' Lincoln's gray, probing stare met Adams'. ''With the first bolt of lightning, the trees will go up like they were soaked in gasoline.''

''So what do we do?'' Adams asked. ''Toward what end do we beard the lion?''

''A controlled burn.''

''You want to convince Gus to set the walnut grove afire to save it from fire?'' Adams knew of this method of burning away underbrush to save mature trees. But convincing Gus was another matter. ''Lotsa luck, fella.''

''Not me.'' Lincoln wagged his head from side to side. ''You, Adams Cade, the first son of Gus Cade.''

"You've gotta be kidding."

"I never kid about fire, or trees, or Gus." Rising from his seat, looking more weary than he would admit, Lincoln added, "You have Gus' ear, at least for now. He'll listen to you."

"Yeah, right," Adams scoffed.

"Yeah, right is right." Squelching a yawn and stretching his rangy body, Lincoln grinned. "Since you guys seem to have everything here under control, I'm going home."

Pausing at the barn door, he tossed a parting shot. "You have to go to Eden's party, Adams. You have no choice."

"Why?" Adams was immediately angry. Everyone seemed to know what should and must be done better than he.

"Because that's the night Jeffie will give her the portrait. You need to be there. If not for Eden's sake, then for Jeffie's. God knows, he's been through enough and deprived himself of enough since you went to prison, without adding the feeling that he's keeping you two apart."

Adams bolted from his seat, his expression contorted. "What the hell does that mean?"

"Exactly what I said." Lincoln didn't pause or turn around. "Be there, Adams. For Jeffie."

"No," Adams shouted to no avail. He was speaking to an empty doorway. Even the paddock was deserted. Jefferson and Jackson were walking the stallion to the creek, cooling him down. Adams was alone with his thoughts. Alone to puzzle over Lincoln's parting comment.

The night of August first, the thud of a solidly delivered blow threatened his bedroom door. But when Adams opened it, he was met by Lincoln's smiling face. The second son was dressed in a formal white shirt, with an untied cravat trailing down his chest. A ruby-red vest and black jacket were lying over one shoulder and anchored by the curl of two fingers. Straightening from the doorjamb, he inspected Adams critically.

"Good," he said, brushing past his older brother as if he'd been invited in. "You're dressed for the occasion. I was hoping I wouldn't have to thrash you first."

"In your dreams, brother." Adams adjusted his black tie, then slipped into his vest and black jacket, which fit his shoulders perfectly.

"I could try." Lincoln advanced a step or two. "When I called your office, your girl Friday said she knew exactly what to send."

"My girl Friday may be yesterday's girl after this stunt." Adams raked a hand through his hair, disturbing the order he'd only recently restored.

"Would you really have missed this, Adams?" Lincoln was as serious as only Lincoln could be. "This is Jeffie's first real portrait. The first time he's really shared with the world what he feels about anyone, and he chose Eden." The piercing gray gaze bored into the depths of Adams' eyes. "Could you miss this moment? If there were ten Junior Rabbs, could you?"

Adams didn't answer at first, then he murmured on a half breath, "No. I wouldn't miss it."

Lincoln's only answer was to slip into his own vest and jacket, shrugging his broad shoulders to settle it properly. Drawing his sleeves over his wrists and adjusting his cuff links, he looked up with a grin. "Ready?"

"Where's Jackson?"

"Fuming impatiently in the car." Crossing the room, Lincoln waited in the doorway, aware that Adams was postponing the inevitable. "Before you ask," he drawled, "Jefferson's gone on ahead. He's to meet Cullen, and together they're going to set up the portrait in a private part of the garden. Where, hopefully, Eden won't see it until time for the unveiling.''

''Wait a minute.'' Adams' eyes narrowed as he wondered if the portrait was a hoax to get him to attend the celebration. ''Eden doesn't know about the portrait?''

''Of course not.'' Lincoln gave his brother the sort of long-suffering look one gives the village fool. ''If she did, how could it be a surprise?''

''Then how did Jeffie paint it? From photographs?''

''Maybe some, but my guess would be that the better part of it he did from memory.'' Realizing Adams hadn't been privy to the quiet, introspective times that often held Jefferson in thrall, Lincoln explained, ''Jeffie sees more with his mind's eye than most of us see with binoculars.''

''He's that good?'' Adams buttoned his vest and adjusted his tie. His gaze caught Lincoln's in the mirror. ''Truly?''

''Better.'' Lincoln grinned. ''Truly. Now, are you coming?''

''Aren't you going to tie your tie?''

Sighing, Lincoln rolled his eyes. ''No, I'm going to find Lady Mary and let her do it. She likes scolding me and complaining that I never seemed to master the art.''

''Like hell, you didn't.'' Adams finally moved to the door.

''So.'' Another shrug lifted the shoulders of Lincoln's impeccable jacket. ''It makes the old girl happy to think I need her. Where's the harm?''

''It's no wonder you were her favorite.''

''Was not.''

''Was too.''

With the resulting laughter still echoing through the rambling house, Lincoln sobered. ''Did I tell you Jericho

and his entire staff will be on guard? Actually,'' he
amended, ''they all would've been there in any case. But
this time they're doing double duty as guests *and* protec-
tors.''

Adams stopped dead in his tracks, facing Lincoln.
''Then Jericho's as worried about this as I am.''

''Jericho's cautious. Not worried. Because he's cautious, he's called in a team from the next county to help
patrol the grounds.'' Anticipating Adams' next question,
Lincoln said, ''The river, too. Does that satisfy you?''

Adams drew a long breath. ''Yes.''

''Good.'' Linking his arm through Adams' arm, Lincoln laughed. ''Now, where were we?''

''Was not, I think.''

''Was too.''

Laughing, the two brothers joined the third in the waiting car. Tonight the eldest of Gus Cade's sons would pay
tribute to the talent of the youngest of them.

Nine

The music reached out to them before they left Jackson's car. Before the reserved young man dressed in proper livery greeted them courteously and took the keys.

"Must be Cullen's handiwork," Lincoln declared as they stood at the entrance to River Walk. The scene before them could have been taken from the canvas of a perfect painting.

"The house, the gardens, the music or the table of food half a mile long?" Jackson drawled.

"All of it. Any takers?" Lincoln looked to either side, challenging his brothers.

"I don't bet against sure things." Jackson grinned.

"What about you, big brother?" Lincoln jostled Adams' arm. When all he got was a blank look, he said, "Why don't you cut to the chase and find Eden? Along the way, if you see Jeffie with his usual coterie of admirers, tell him we'll gravitate to Cullen's punch bowl in an hour or so."

"Yes. I think I will." Without further comment, Adams wandered away, his gaze searching the distant garden, seeking one face among the few who were just beginning to gather there.

"Do you think he heard a word of that?" Lincoln asked Jackson as the two of them watched Adams cross the lawn completely oblivious to the interested looks that followed him.

"Nah. Not once you got past the part about finding Eden." Jackson was already selecting the first of his dancing partners. "But Jeffie will find us. And I'm sure Lady Mary is waiting for you." He left Lincoln to fend for himself as the first of his choices arrived.

The gardens that segued one into another were separate sections of the same sprawling space, with every inch of each section groomed to picture-book perfection. But Adams was too preoccupied to notice the gardens. Nor did he notice the flirtatious sidelong glances the female half of the early arrivals cast his way, many turning for a longer second look as he passed by with only a pleasant greeting. It was Jericho who caught his attention with a long-held look, assuring him all was well. And well guarded.

Then Adams saw her. Eden, more lovely than he remembered, wearing a gown that was the stuff of dreams. A sleek, regal column, the beguiling hue of river mist at sunset. Lavender, yet darker, and more luminous than violet. Like a richly glowing sheath of gossamer, the clinging fabric shaped her breasts, nipped in at her waist, then flowed discreetly over slim hips to fall to her ankles. Straps so thin they might have been illusion held a discreetly provocative décolletage.

She wore her hair gathered in a mass of loose curls at her crown, with tendrils beginning to tumble from the clasp of pearls, amethyst and gold. A sophisticated style, yet inviting his touch, as the golden-brown strands skimmed over her bare shoulders, teasing all the scented places Adams longed to kiss.

But even as drifting curls made their alluring declaration, there was more. An exquisitely matched string of pearls banded by matching beads of amethyst and gold flowed from her neck to her waist in muted radiance. And as pearls and gold and stone caressed her breasts with each subtle sway of her body, no man who still lived could forget that beneath the elegance and the polish, Eden Claibourne was all woman.

Obviously no man had, and Adams felt the insidious twist of jealousy as he watched one gallant after another kiss her cheek or her hand. An older, distinguished gentleman sent jealousy spiraling into anger by kissing her first, then drawing her into a long embrace. It did nothing to soothe his temper that the gentleman greeted a number of ladies in the same fashion.

Threading his way through what had quickly become a crowd, he acknowledged salutations with the dismissive charm that had served him well in many tense boardroom exchanges. Deftly resisting being drawn into conversations, he arrived at last to stand before Eden.

"Adams!" Her face was alight with pleasure. "You came. I thought you wouldn't. I was afraid you would think you shouldn't."

"I tried not to come. I knew I shouldn't." He smiled ruefully, unable to take his gaze from her.

"I'm glad." Eden reached out to take his hands. Stifling a sharply indrawn breath, she turned them in hers, studying his palms and the calluses that were spawning

calluses, the bruises, the torn nails and the angry scratch
along one thumb. When she released him at last and lifted
her eyes to meet his, there was a mist of tears gathering
on her lashes. "Your poor hands. Jefferson said you were
stringing fences on the back pastures, hoping cattle might
provide a steady revenue."

"We have been. We are," Adams said as he dared
brush a gentle fingertip over her lashes. Catching a droplet
that glistened like a jewel against his skin and folding the
minute bit of moisture into his palm, he murmured,
"Sweetheart, there's nothing wrong with my hands that
hasn't been wrong with them before. More times than I
can remember."

"I know." Eden's voice was unsteady, barely more
than a whisper. "I just wasn't prepared—"

The string quartet chose that moment to end a short
break. The music was soft, as perfect an accompaniment
for the gala and for Eden as the garden setting.

"I should leave you to your guests." Adams intended
to distance himself from her. Instead, on impulse, he drew
her to him, his head dipping to hers. His breath was warm
on her face as he whispered, "Happy birthday, my beautiful Eden."

He meant only to graze her cheek with his lips, but in
a slow, mesmerizing turn of her head, Eden offered her
mouth. A temptation too sweet to resist, anywhere, anytime.

His lips brushed hers, hungering but not daring to take
more. As he drew away, Eden's fingers curled at his neck,
keeping him. "Stay. Stay with me tonight."

Adam's heart quickened. The force of it threatened the
wall of his chest. "No, Eden."

The palm of her free hand curved around his mouth.
"Just for the duration of the party." Her look was plead-

ing. "I know you're convinced people will talk. I know you don't want them to link you to me. But they will, Adams. No matter what we do.

"What the gossips don't see or hear, they'll invent. So why not let them speak the truth when it's time to gossip?" Her fingers traced the shape of his lips in a caress as tempting as a kiss. "Are a few rumors a price too dear to pay for an innocent evening spent in each other's company? We were friends most of our lives. Can't we be friends again? Just friends. Just for tonight?"

She fell silent, waiting, never looking away from Adams. For Eden there was no one else in the garden. This was her birthday, and the answer he might give could be the best gift of all.

All she needed was there in her eyes, in the soft shape of her mouth. Only a fool couldn't see. Only a fool would refuse.

Adams Cade had been many things. A fool wasn't one of them. "Yes, love." The words were little more that the stirring of a breath. "I'll stay. Until the last guest is gone, I'll stay."

Eden's smile, the warmth of her touch as she slid her hand into the bend of the arm he offered, was worth any risk. But, Adams wondered, would he agree at another, saner time?

"A number of your old classmates are here. Cullen has already warned me that most of them are anxious to speak with you." She looked up at him in the flicker of candlelight just gaining strength as twilight began its descent into darkness. "Would you mind so much?"

"I don't mind." He'd expected he would, but unwise as it was, with Eden at his side, matters of lamentable proportions were insignificant. "Who's here? I've seen Jericho, of course."

"Come with me, Adams, and I'll show you." She moved with him, a vision dressed in twilight. Her fingers curved in subtle possession at his elbow. The softness of her breasts brushing his arm was a whisper of enchantment and remembered madness. Her laughter was low, unconsciously seductive. For the first time in weeks and for this little time, Eden Claibourne was happy.

As they strolled along the edge of the crowd, Eden named names, telling him a little about each person she identified. But in the end, Adams matched faces to names without erring.

"Blaine." Hands met in a delighted slap of flesh against flesh as he encountered the first of a number of old friends after too many years. "How are you? How is little Melanie? Though I don't suppose she's so little anymore."

Eden was younger, but she remembered that Blaine Ellington and a girl she couldn't recall married young and had a baby girl before graduating from high school. And it was obvious that Adams recalled everything.

Blaine answered, plainly flattered that Adams remembered. "She's nineteen."

"Nineteen?" Adams' brows lifted. "I know it's a cliché, but they do grow up fast. And Cindy?"

"We divorced ten years ago. Neither Melanie nor I have had contact with her since."

That first conversation set the pattern. Everyone was eager to speak with him. No one presumed. No one judged. Adams was tireless and remained faultless in his recognition and recollections. The party became a subtle celebration of the return of Adams Cade, and he was too gracious to interrupt the stream of well-wishers or those who came to reminisce. It was Eden who finally called a halt.

"I think this is my dance." Slipping a hand into one of Adams', she turned a blinding smile on the gathered group. "If you will excuse us?"

Eden led him to the courtyard square. As she went into his arms, her body moving with his, the smile she saved for him was poignant and tender. "They love you, Adams. No one judges you. Not one of the old friends you met tonight believes you could be capable of what Junior Rabb claimed and accused you of. I saw it in their faces and heard it in their voices."

"What you saw was Lady Mary's teaching coming to the fore." Holding her close, he swung her into a graceful turn, released her and drew her back, keeping her a bit closer.

"Lady Mary's good work aside, it was more than that."

"Sweetheart." His head bent to hers. His lips skimmed her brow. "Do me a favor."

"Anything."

"Shut up and let me dance, just with you."

Eden's heart skipped a beat with the suggestive innuendo. Then, delighted, she threw back her head and laughed, drawing all eyes to them. "Indeed, yes." Softly, her cheek brushing the lapel of his jacket, she whispered, "It would be my pleasure, dear sir."

"No, love," Adams said as their bodies moved in concert, so closely the gown of dark, misty lavender was only the prelude to seduction. "The pleasure is mine."

If any attention hadn't been riveted on them, Eden's laughter drew it now, like a magnet. Even Cullen and Merrie and the rest of the wait staff paused to watch.

At that particular moment, the rest of the Cades had shaken free of their respective adoring coteries and gathered at a table apart. A table bearing, along with a massive flower arrangement, a spectacular bowl filled with Cullen's punch. An exotic, gleaming liquid so darkly red it was almost black.

"Look at them," Jackson said as he held a cup inches from his mouth and nose. "They move together like one person."

"Like they belong together," Lincoln added.

"As they should have been for the past thirteen years." Jefferson's voice was strained, bitter, but neither Lincoln nor Jackson commented.

"What's with you, Jeffie?" Jackson asked around a first swallow of punch that almost choked him. When he could speak again, it was to say to Jefferson, "You should be dancing. Lord knows, you wouldn't lack for partners, if you'd give the ladies a second look."

"Not tonight." With a grimace, Jefferson brushed off the remark. "Too many butterflies. I keep wondering what Eden will say when Cullen unveils the portrait. What if she hates it?"

"She won't." Lincoln snagged a cup from the table, deciding to brave the punch since Jackson was still on his feet.

"You can't say that for sure any more than I can," Jefferson shot back.

"Yes, we can." Jackson tried another sip, which went down more easily. Smiling lazily and swirling the dark-ruby liquid in the delicate crystal, he looked back at Jefferson. "Lincoln and I are far better judges of your work than you are."

"Right." Lincoln's voice was raw as he pressed a hand against his stomach as if expecting a hole to appear at any moment. "You're concerned—it's natural. But if you take a few sips of Cullen's witch-doctor brew, I guarantee you won't have any butterflies. Fried ones, maybe. But nothing fluttering."

Jefferson laughed then, and his mood eased as both brothers intended. This repartee, or one similar, accompanied the first sips of Cullen's special punch at each of the last seven birthdays Eden had celebrated at River Walk.

Filling his cup to capacity, Jefferson drank it in one effort. Keeping his face straight, and in a voice almost unaffected, he teased, "If you can't take it, good brothers, there's a table or two along the way. One even has lemonade."

Then he grimaced, his startlingly handsome face twisting in a mask of horror. "But you're right, Lincoln. No butterflies. Now it's the flames of Hades, instead."

"But you love it. You're even safe, as long as it doesn't eat through the crystal." Cullen stepped into their midst, towering over even Lincoln by half a foot. "Also, you're all right about one thing or another."

In a rare breach of his own etiquette, Cullen filled a cup for himself and drank it as if it were water. Setting the cup down and wiping his mouth, he reiterated, "Yes, Adams and Mistress Eden do move like one. Yes, they belong together. Yes, if circumstances had been different, they should have been together all these years. But I wouldn't be here, then. And we wouldn't be unveiling this portrait tonight." Taking a watch from his pocket, he returned it after a glance. "Right now."

"You're ready?" Jefferson realized he was wrong— the butterflies had survived the witch doctor's brew.

"Give us five minutes," Cullen said. "Then get your brother and Mistress and come along."

When the islander left them, moving through the crowd like a rogue wave among ripples, Jackson drawled in a lazy tone, "Cullen must have tasted the punch a little too much as he was mixing it. He's positively loquacious tonight. I don't think I've heard him say that many words at one time since he came to Belle Terre with Eden.''

'''Loquacious'?'' Lincoln rolled his eyes and winked at Jefferson. ''He must not be the only one affected by the punch. Did our brother say 'loquacious'?''

''Aw, guys,'' Jackson protested. ''It's a good word.''

''And a long one.'' Jefferson was smiling once again, as his brothers intended.

By word of mouth or by magic—Adams never knew for certain—the celebrants began to gravitate toward a particularly secluded part of the gardens. Where, cloistered by giant oaks weeping with Spanish moss and alight with torches turning evening to midday, an easel of dark wood waited. Flanked by clusters of clipped hollies and pots of heavy-headed hydrangeas, its drape of midnight velvet captured the flickering light, drawing cries of appreciation from the ladies.

But no one was more awestruck than Eden. She turned to Adams as if he knew the answers to dozens of unasked questions. But he only gave a small nod and a lift of his brows in innocence. Even Jefferson appeared equally uninformed as Cullen stepped forward to stand with one hand resting on the easel.

''Once in a great while a beautiful creature and a great talent come together in the same place and time.'' The islander's gaze touched on Jefferson, then on Eden. ''When that unique meeting occurs, we are blessed with great pleasures such as this.

''Ladies and gentlemen, Eden Roberts Claibourne, as painted by Thomas Jefferson Cade,'' Cullen said simply as he drew the drape from the easel, revealing a girl wrapped in the magic of a misty garden. A young girl in a white, flowing gown, almost, yet not quite, a woman.

A girl with tousled golden curls and the wonder of love in her soft gray eyes. Eden, as she'd looked on the night of her debut. Before Adams had been taken from her.

After one collective gasp, the garden was quiet. Then the whispers began, and the applause.

Eden stood rooted, her hand clasping Adams', her gaze seeking Jefferson. Then, with a smile from Adams, she was crossing the little space separating her from Jefferson. Taking his hands in both of hers, she rose on tiptoe to kiss his cheek.

"Thank you," she whispered as she drew away. "It's beautiful. I've never looked so beautiful."

"You did. You would, if the past were different." Jefferson's gaze met hers. "You can now, if you make it happen."

"You know, don't you?"

"That you love my brother?" Jefferson inclined his head only slightly, his smile bittersweet. "I've always known."

"You painted me as you thought I would look if all the dreams I've dreamed could come true."

"I painted the girl who became a woman who goes on with her life, and yet waits for her lover to make her complete." His grasp tightened over hers. "It can be, Eden. All that's gone on before tonight could be resolved if Adams would—"

"Jefferson!" Lady Mary tapped him on the shoulder with her cane, ending the conversation. "Well—" the small lady peered up at him intensely "—have I not preached for years that you're wasting a God-given talent by burying yourself in the swamps?"

A palsied wave recalled Jefferson's attention to Eden's portrait. "Does this not prove my point?"

Eden heard no more as she was drawn into a circle of

curious friends. "No, I didn't pose for the painting." She addressed the most common questions. "And yes, I was as surprised as anyone."

Over the heads of those who gathered around her, Eden smiled at Adams. A smile that took his breath away. A smile that drew his gaze back to the portrait where Eden looked out on the world exactly as she'd just looked at him.

A smile that sent all his good intentions into nothing. With ill-disguised unrest, he waited and he watched. Until Jefferson joined him. "Well, brother," Jefferson said in low tones, "what do you think?"

Throwing an arm around the younger man's shoulders, Adams drew him into a hard, quick embrace. "I think you've one helluva talent, Jeffie, and Lady Mary is right—you're wasting it by burying yourself in the swamp, and even at Belle Reve."

"Where else would I go, Adams?" Jefferson's expression was instantly grim. "What else can I do?"

"No, Jeffie." Adams clasped a hand around his brother's neck, shaking him gently, as if he could shake reason into him. "The question is, what can't you do? If you stop locking yourself and your talent away from the world."

"Gus needed me. He still needs me."

"Gus is on the mend. He was lucky this time. If he takes better care of himself, there's a good chance there won't be another stroke. Particularly since Belle Reve is solvent and back in good repair."

"Thanks to you, Adams. With your hard work and the money from the merger you poured into the coffers of Belle Reve, you've made it right again." Jefferson looked from the portrait to Eden, then back to Adams. "As you've always done, at great cost to your own dreams."

"That means you aren't allowed your own? That you can't have what you dream about?" Adams knew he was losing the battle. And this wasn't the time or place for more persuasive discussions. "Never mind, I know your answer. But look at what you've done. The most modest man in the world would admit there's amazing talent in Eden's portrait.

"Lincoln and Jackson said she didn't pose, and probably there were no photos. You did this from memory." Adams cast an admiring glance in the direction of the portrait. Even her picture could set his heart racing. "I don't know how you managed it with so little time, yet you captured something remarkable and unique."

"I painted her as I know she would look if we could put the past behind us," Jefferson declared quietly.

"I think maybe we can, Jeffie." Adams placed a hand on Jefferson's shoulder. "Junior's been quiet for so long I've begun to hope the vandalism of the cottage was his one great act of bravado. I've found myself thinking maybe he's realized his vendetta isn't worth its cost.

"This party, with the reception I've been given by the people who matter, and now the portrait, your portrait of Eden, have shown me that, just maybe, I can come home again."

"Gus' attitude hasn't changed, Adams. Even as hard as you've worked, and with his suspicions about the source of the money, he hasn't changed how he feels about you."

"It matters," Adams admitted. "I won't tell you it doesn't. But one opinion, even that of the father who labeled me an outcast, isn't the most important factor in my life, at last."

"No." Jefferson smiled. "The important factor in your life is standing by the fountain. If you've got half the sense I think, you won't keep her waiting another minute.''

"I second that motion." Jackson flung an arm around the shoulders of the youngest and the oldest of his brothers. "In fact, if I had someone like Eden waiting for me, I would run, not walk, to the nearest—"

"Whoa, Red, there may be delicate ears about." Lincoln completed the circle. "But I do make the motion unanimous.''

"Then what am I waiting for?" Adams wondered aloud.

"Beats me," Jackson, ever the one to have the last word, drawled and grinned.

Eden had managed to extricate herself from the crowd that had gathered around her and the portrait. For a while Jefferson answered questions regarding the painting. After he excused himself, leaving the limelight solely to Eden, there was little she could add. Yet she couldn't quite convince the determinedly curious that she'd known nothing of this wonderful gift. Ultimately, though, even the most persistent admitted defeat and let her walk away.

Now she stood alone by a small fountain, letting the sound of the water and the mesmerizing motion fill the waiting with a measure of peace. Adams hands spanning her waist, drawing her back against him, came as no surprise. She'd known he would come. From the moment he'd looked at her as she stood by the portrait, it was for this she waited.

As she leaned into his embrace, she realized the expensive scent of the staid and scrupulously groomed businessman was no more. The too-proper man who felt he must prove himself and his worth to the world in every way was gone at last.

This was Adams, still splendid, still wonderful, a little less perfect. Adams, with his dark hair not quite so neat, his expression not so controlled. Adams, who smelled of fresh air, lingering sunshine and a hint of soap. Adams.

"I know it's your party," he murmured into her hair, "but do you suppose we could shock the good citizens of Belle Terre by ducking out for a while?"

Turning in his embrace, Eden linked her hands at his nape. "I thought you'd never ask."

"Know anyplace in particular?" He teased a drifting curl with a soft breath.

"Cullen suggested you might like to see the refurbishing we've done to the river cottage."

"The river cottage, huh?" Adams' smile was in his voice.

"Just in case you might, he left a bottle of champagne cooling in the bedroom." There was matching laughter in Eden. "To toast my birthday."

"Ah, yes, your birthday. I didn't buy you a gift." He kissed her eyes, her nose, the corners of her mouth. But when she would have returned his kisses, he drew away. "Can you forgive me?"

"I'm sure we'll think of some way you might redeem yourself." Eden let her hands slide over the pleats of his shirt and down his vest. Slipping her arm around him, she walked with him along the sheltered path to the cottage.

Neither saw Cullen step from the shadows, smile his rare smile and station himself squarely in the path Eden and Adams had taken. An immovable force no one would challenge.

Adams expected a twinge of grief for the destruction he'd brought down on the cottage. But the repairs were too complete and the night too splendid for regret of any sort.

"Your father's collections." Taking first one decoy from a shelf and then another, he inspected each. "As good as before."

"Cullen found someone to restore them." Eden moved to his side, thankful Cullen understood it would be good for Adams to see the vandal had done no lasting harm. "He found others to restore the paintings and even the fabrics. The glass and a few insignificant objects were all that couldn't be restored or repaired. So, your former abode, my dear Adams." A slow, sweeping gesture accompanied the endearment. "Yes, as good as before.

"But—" a tilt of her head sent another lock tumbling from the clasp in her hair "—must we spend what's left of the evening discussing the cottage?" Tossing him a mischievous smile, she crossed to the bedroom door. "If you can't think of anything better, I'll have a glass of champagne. Talking is thirsty work."

"We have a few things to discuss other than the cottage." Catching her wrist, he drew her back to him. "Such as this."

Looping a finger under a corded strap of her gown, he traced its path from her shoulder to the swell of her breasts. "Do they serve a purpose, or are they merely tantalizing decoration?"

"Oh, they have a purpose, I assure you." Eden shivered as his knuckle traced the same path as before, ending again only inches from the tips of her breasts.

"Something to drive me mad, like the dress?" he suggested softly. "That was the reason for this intriguing bit of lavender, was it not? To fascinate and entice, until I couldn't remember any promise I'd made to myself. Was that it, my love?"

"Yes." Her voice was breathless. The pulse at her temple and her throat told him she had been caught in her own web.

"And now, sweet Eden? When your spell is complete, what now?" Abandoning the whimsical straps, his fingertips danced across the edge of the bodice of her gown, tarrying at the cleft of her breasts to stroke the silky flesh of their rising curves. When she shivered and caught back a moan, he chuckled in wicked delight. "A weaver of magic caught in a spell of her own making? I wonder, what must she do?"

"This." As he had, she looped a finger beneath one lavender strap and then the other. With her arms crossed over her breasts and her palms moving in tantalizing increments down her arms, she slipped the dress from her body. When it dropped to the floor in a bright, shimmering puddle, she wore only pearls and a G-string of the sort that had left her body tanned and little marred. As slowly, as provocatively, never taking her gaze from his, Eden lifted her hands to her hair.

"Let me." Not moving, Adams awaited her answer.

Eden let her hands fall to her sides. She stood, unabashed, beneath the plundering possession of his gaze. As before, the time for modesty had long passed.

Adams opened the clasp, letting her hair slip free. Loose curls of darkly burnished gold tumbled around her shoulders, down her back and over her breasts. Tangling his fingers in the gleaming mane, he tilted her face to his, taking her mouth in a deep, waiting kiss. Then he was touching her, stroking her hair, caressing her face, her throat, her body. A slight hesitation at her waist, and the last scrap of clothing that hid her from his possession fell away.

"Eden." Only her name, but as much part of his mind-shattering kiss as his suckling lips.

With her last shred of sanity, Eden whispered in quiet joy, "You aren't leaving. You wouldn't be here, you wouldn't be touching me, you wouldn't be making love to me, if you were."

"No, love." Adams swept her into his arms. "I'm not going anywhere but to the bedroom, with you."

"This is your gift to me?"

"Yes," he promised. "And to myself."

In a darkened room, far from the merrymakers and the revelers, an outcast learned he wasn't an outcast, and would never be, as long as there was love in the eyes and the heart of the only person who'd ever really mattered. In her arms a once gentle man, who learned to be harsh and hard in a world that demanded it as the price of survival, discovered that the gentleness in him truly hadn't died.

As she drew him down to her, he believed, at last, that the man he might have been had only waited for her tender touch, her sweet kiss and her unquestioning trust to live again.

As he believed in her caress he found peace.

In her murmured, "I love you, Adams," breathed against his lips, he found his soul.

In the sweet welcome of her body he found hope and dreams of the future.

Eden was his future and all he would ever want.

"Yes, Eden," he whispered from the depths of a healing heart. "My only love."

Ten

"**W**hat the devil!" Adams nearly stood on the brakes, sending the car into a skid only an expert hand could have saved. When Jackson's vehicle rocked to a stop, Jackson, Jefferson and Lincoln were staring with him at a red sky at midnight.

Eden's party had ended at midnight, and Adams was made designated driver and butt of all teasing. Now everyone was cold sober and deadly serious.

"Fire," Lincoln whispered. "A big one."

"River Trace or the barn." Jackson's terse response was strained through taut lips. "Maybe both."

"The horses." Jefferson voiced the anguish of all.

"Maybe it's not too late." His foot to the floor, Adams sped down the road. When he made the final turn into River Trace, towering flames licked the night sky.

They could hear the horses' frantic screams before Adams halted the car by the inferno. The barn was in full blaze. Miraculously, with weather that turned the country-side to tinder, the house was unharmed.

As they exited the car with doors flung open, a few steps made it clear the cries of the horses didn't come from the barn. Jackson pointed to a pasture where his animals reared and raced along fences.

Spinning around, he stared at the barn, a burning skeleton. "Somebody saved them. The whole herd."

"*That* somebody!" Adams shouted above the crash of falling timbers, drawing their attention back to the house.

"Merrie." Jefferson was the first to reach her. Taking the hose from her, he kept the spray on the house. "Are you hurt?"

Obviously exhausted, Eden's young charge cried out her assurance over the furor. Then there was no more time for conversation or explanations. The horses were safe. The barn was beyond saving. But the house could go yet. As they joined in the fight, the Cades knew Merrie's efforts were heroic, but might have only delayed the inevitable in the battle still ahead.

"Why were you here?" The barn was a smoldering pyre. Jackson and Lincoln were checking the horses, and Adams sat at the kitchen table, cleaning a burn on Merrie Alexandre's wrist. "Lucky for Jackson that you were. But why?"

"I like horses better than parties." Merrie shrugged prettily despite the layer of soot that covered her. "When my duties were done at the inn, I came to talk to the horses. I hope Mr. Jackson doesn't mind."

Jefferson set a glass of cold water before her. "Mind? I would think he's more in the mood to kiss you."

"No, thank you." Merrie shook her head, sending curls

flying from the bandanna that had protected her hair. ''I don't care for kissing.''

''Unless it's a horse,'' Adams ventured with a smile.

The wail of a siren forestalled Merrie's reply.

''The local fire department, and unless I miss my guess, Jericho won't be far behind.'' Jefferson slid the glass closer to the girl. ''Better drink this. You'll be explaining all over again about being in the stall with the stallion and hearing, but not seeing, whoever it was that started the fire.

''Jericho's thorough—he'll want every detail.'' Jefferson grimaced as he remembered Merrie's story. ''Down to the cut telephone lines, how you managed to coax a stable of frightened horses from a burning barn. And why you thought to keep the hose on the house to prevent it from going up in smoke like the barn.''

''You're exhausted, Merrie. I'll fill him in as best I can. Then the questioning will go quicker for you.'' Adams laid aside the ointment scavenged from Jackson's medicine cabinet, patted Merrie's shoulder and left the table. His weary look met his brother's over her dark head. ''Jefferson?''

''I'll look after her, Adams.'' Jefferson's steady regard didn't falter. ''Go meet Jericho. Tell him what he needs to know.''

Thirteen days later Jericho tossed the report detailing the fire at River Trace on his desk. ''Every expert at our disposal crawled over Jackson's barn for weeks. The final analysis tells the what, where and how of the fire. But not who started it.''

''We know who started it, Jericho.'' Adams stared out a window that looked over the main street of Belle Terre.

"What we know doesn't matter, Adams. I can't arrest Junior Rabb without proof."

"So he'll just keep striking out at me and anyone close to me as long as I'm here. Always with his iron-clad alibi."

"He'll trip up," Jericho declared in a low growl. "Sooner or later he'll make a mistake."

"Maybe, but I can't take the chance he might hurt someone before sooner or later comes."

"Your family," Jericho supplied. "And Eden."

Adams didn't look away from the window. "I worry most about her. My brothers can take care of themselves."

"Eden has Cullen. He would be a powerful deterrent even for a swamp rat like Junior Rabb. But," Jericho added thoughtfully, "he can't be with her every minute of every day."

"There's a better solution." Adams crossed to the desk, faced Jericho squarely. "One I should have taken weeks ago."

"Leave Belle Terre." As sheriff, Jericho knew this was the logical conclusion. Rabb had bothered none of the Cades until Adams came home. "What about Gus and the plantation?"

"Gus is improving daily. Once the hospital sent out nurses he couldn't bully and he started behaving himself, his progress has been phenomenal. Belle Reve's solvent for the moment. And, as ironic as it sounds, after a controlled burn, in a year or two enough timber can be harvested off some of the back acres to keep a sensibly managed operation going for years."

Adams shrugged, his face was grim. "I could have left weeks ago, but I thought—"

"Eden," Jericho called her name, explaining everything.

"Yeah." Adams looked again to the window. "Eden."

"Have you told her?"

"I've only seen her once since the fire. She came to River Trace. I asked her not to come again."

"So when will you tell her?"

"I'm leaving tomorrow. I'll tell her then."

The chair squeaked as Jericho leaned forward. "A little abrupt, isn't it? This is going to hurt her enough as it is."

"I know." Adams stared at his fisted hands as if he didn't know what to do with them. "Short of going after Rabb and risking that the added strain might kill my father, there's nothing else I can do. The quicker I go, the quicker the vendetta will end."

"Goes against the grain, walking away from a fight, doesn't it? I can't recall that you ever started a fight in the old days. But you sure as hell never walked away from one." Jericho watched Adams closely, hoping for a reaction that never came.

"This isn't the old days. There's more at stake than what I want. For the sake of the innocents, my only option is to say goodbye. Starting now." Extending his hand, Adams smiled wryly when the sheriff's large hand engulfed his briefly. "You're the only person I know who's bigger than Cullen. Will you help him take care of her?"

"You know I will."

"I guess I do." Adams opened the office door.

"Adams." Jericho waited until he had his friend's undivided attention. "You never stopped by for that talk I wanted to have about the night all this with Junior Rabb began."

"There was no need, Jericho. It's all in the report. I don't have anything to add." Adams smiled one last time, a smile that didn't touch his eyes, and closed the door behind him.

* * *

Adams paused on the walk, staring up at the marvelous old house. Once River Walk had belonged to Eden's ancestors. This street of old houses had been the showplace of wealthy planters' infidelity. Fancy Row, named for the scandalous reputation of the ladies who occupied them, not the architecture.

Belle Terre was steeped in its own history, with a character of its own. He would miss it. Where else would a man with the pompous name of Caesar Augustus Cade name his sons after John Quincy Adams, Abraham Lincoln, Andrew Jackson and Thomas Jefferson? "Where but in a land that could spawn a town like Belle Terre?"

Adams hadn't expected to fall in love again in Belle Terre. Or with it. But he had. He never expected to regret leaving it. Yet he did. He must. And it was time.

Crossing the walk, he climbed the steps. At the door he halted. It was morning. The gardens would be drenched with dew. Eden would be gathering flowers. Descending the steps, he circled the house and opened the garden gate. Eden was there, a basket of freshly cut hydrangeas swinging from her wrist. Her image was imprinted in his memory, yet he always forgot how beautiful she was. Only in the eye of the beholder, she would scoff. But to this beholder, who loved her more than life, she was beautiful.

"Adams?" Her voice was breathless and pleased at once. Then she saw the perfect suit, the perfect tie. The too rigidly perfect man who had taken her lover's place.

The basket fell to the ground. Lavender and rose-colored blooms spilled at her feet. Adams saw the color wash from her face, and tears mist her eyes.

"You've come to say goodbye."

"Yes." Adams flinched. It hurt to see her like this.

"Why?" Before he could answer, she shook her head.

Her hair was down this morning and just beginning to curl in the damp morning air. "I hoped..."

"What, sweetheart?" Adams voice was ragged. His nails scoured his palms against his need to touch her.

"It doesn't matter." Her head was down as she stared at broken flowers. Then she lifted her gaze to his. "I won't ask if you love me. I know you do. I won't ask why you feel you must leave. I didn't want to admit it, but I've known since the fire you would go. To protect those you love from Junior Rabb's vendetta."

"If there was another way..."

"But there isn't," Eden finished. "Without causing more grief for your father." Bitterness crept in. "A man who used you unmercifully, yet can't forgive what he thinks you did.

"I won't ever believe it, Adams. No matter what you say or what Junior Rabb claims, I won't ever believe you could be capable of an unprovoked attack." The bitterness was gone, and the defeat. She was magnificent in the morning sun, magnificent in her trust and belief in him.

"That's a finished chapter, Eden. Nothing can change it."

"I can." Junior Rabb stepped away from the trunk of a massive oak, his glare wild and feral. Raising a rifle to his shoulder, he set his sights on Adams. "Now."

"No!" Eden cried, and took a step toward Rabb.

"Eden. Don't," Adams said quietly, catching her wrist, keeping her close. Even as he marveled at her courage, he felt an oppressive regret that she'd drawn Rabb's attention.

Adams had seen madness in the face marked by the livid scar left by the blow that had changed all their lives. The killing madness he'd witnessed too often in prison to mistake for mere anger. Though pitiful comfort, it solved the mystery of why Rabb should suddenly go on his rampage. The man, a product of brutality and inbreeding, had likely teetered on the brink of madness for years. Adams' return, the long-standing hatred and bitter envy it recalled, was surely the final push that had sent him over the edge.

There would be no reasoning with him, but Adams had to try. "You don't want to do this, Junior."

"Don't I?" The rifle wavered.

"We know you destroyed the river cottage and torched Jackson's barns. But we have no proof. If you do this, there will be witnesses. People who saw you come here."

"If you're talking about Sheriff Rivers' watchdog, forget him. I drowneded him. But if you're talking about this lady here, now I know how it is between you, I got plans for her."

Still shackling her wrist with his circling fingers, Adams stepped in front of Eden. "Let her go, Junior. She won't say anything. I give you my word."

Rabb's bark of laughter was hoarse and loud. "Gonna protect your lady like you did that piss-ant little brother of yourn? Gonna come riding hell-for-leather to the rescue?

"Know what I think?" The rifle barrel wavered as Rabb sought a second target, but found Eden too well shielded by Adams. "Now I know how it is between you, you was gonna watch her die." Bulky shoulders lifted, stretching a dirty plaid shirt over a bulging belly. "But no matter. I can do it this way. You first, Cade. Your fancy lady second."

Rabb was enjoying the sound of his own voice. Adams saw it as Eden's chance. "When I release you, hit the ground, Eden," he whispered through stiff lips. "Don't hesitate, don't look up.

"Your word, Eden," he demanded before she could question.

"Shut up!" The rifle wavered again, a grimy finger convulsed on the trigger. But it didn't matter, Adams had the promise he sought in the squeeze of Eden's hand.

"You're a fool, Junior." He was baiting Rabb. Twice in his agitation, the hate-filled man had lost his aim. Adams could only hope for a third time. "An even bigger fool than I thought."

"Which one of us went to prison?" Rabb cackled, but the name-calling hit a nerve. Launching into a crowing tirade, he recounted the night of the fight. "The kid snuck through the swamp into Rabb Town. Thought he would 'count *coup*' like some damned redskin, but got hisself caught, instead. I woulda cut his throat and fed him to the gaters, along with his horse, and no one would ever a knowed. Then big brother come riding in hell-for-leather and got hisself a prison sentence, instead. So, who's the fool?"

"You are. *Now*." The rifle had wavered. The last was a command meant for Eden as Adams flung her aside and launched himself at Junior Rabb.

Eden heard the shot as she sprawled facedown, her head crashing against the concrete pad of a sundial. Then the garden was quiet and still. The sun grew dark.

Eden moved restlessly. She tried to open her eyes, but they were weighted, too heavy. She struggled harder.

"Shh, shh." A touch soothed her. "Easy, sweetheart."

Sweetheart. "Adams." She bolted upright and the move brought lightning slicing through her skull. Her lashes lifted at last, but all she saw was a sea of white. "Adams!"

"No, Eden. Not Adams, Jefferson."

She recognized the white sea as a hospital room and the starched linens of a hospital bed. Then she remembered the garden, Junior Rabb and Adams. "Is he...?"

"Adams is in surgery, but he'll be all right. So will you, as soon as a minor concussion and some bruises heal."

"Junior?"

"He's in custody and raving like a maniac. In his delusion he's spilling the whole story. Bragging about what he was going to do to me the night Adams followed me to Rabb Town." Taking her by the shoulders, he leaned her back against the pillows, then folded her hand in both of his. "It's over, Eden. The truth can finally be told, and Adams can come home to stay."

"Tell me about Adams."

"He took a bullet in the shoulder. I won't lie to you, it was a close call. But he took Junior down. He was more concerned with keeping you safe than with his own life. But thanks to Cullen's quick first aid, he's going to be fine. I promise."

"When can I see him?" The throb in her head wouldn't ease. But that Adams lived was all that mattered.

"The minute we get the okay, I'll take you to him."

Now that she could think again, she saw how haggard the youngest Cade was. "You're exhausted, Jefferson."

"Long day." He grinned crookedly. "Not one to repeat."

"Lincoln? Jackson?"

"We're all here. Cullen, too. Even Hobie Verey and Gus. Hobie's called Gus every kind of fool and told Jericho and everybody he saw me ride toward Rabb Town while he was night fishing. And that later Adams rode by, trailing my horse.

"Hobie says he never told anything to anyone, because

if this was how the damn fool Cades wanted it, that was their business. From the first, I wanted to confess that I cracked Junior's skull. But Adams was afraid it would kill Gus to know his favorite…'' Jefferson's voice drifted away in disgust.

"He was probably right," Eden assured him. "And Adams doesn't regret it, Jeffie." Squeezing his hand, she smiled into his glittering blue gaze. "Now that I understand, neither do I."

"But it didn't need to be this way for you and Adams."

"Who's to say this isn't the best way? We might not have ever realized what we have, if we hadn't lost it first."

"Can you forgive me? You don't think I was a coward?"

"You were young. This was Adams' decision. There's nothing cowardly, nor anything to forgive. Except in Gus' case."

Jefferson grinned at the last. "Gus would like to speak with you, if you feel up to it."

"Does he know?"

"That Adams followed his favorite son into Rabb Town? That it was the favorite who struck the fateful blow? He knows. Hobie made sure, remember? Now, after years of denying Adams any compassion or forgiveness, Gus is wondering if Adams can forgive him. That's what he wants to talk to you about."

"I'll see him." Eden caught a sharp breath as shards of pain splintered through her brain and her eyes. "But not just yet. First I want to hear the story of that night, this time from beginning to end. The entire sequence of events."

As Jefferson began to speak, she closed her eyes and, in her mind, rode to Rabb Town with Adams.

* * *

"Hello." Adams' voice and his fingers stroking the tangles from her hair woke Eden. As she raised her head from the edge of his bed, he touched her face. "I thought I dreamed you."

"I'm not a dream, Adams." Sliding her palm into his, she brought his bruised knuckles to her lips. "Thank you, my love."

"For what?" He was pale from loss of blood and hours of surgery, but he managed a cynical smile. "For putting you in danger that almost killed you?"

"No." Eden left the chair where she'd dozed for hours waiting for Adams to awake. Bending over him, she brushed back his hair and let her fingertips linger on the heated flesh of his temple. "For being Adams Cade. For my life. For all our lives."

Her voice dropped a note. "We know, Adams. What Junior Rabb hasn't ranted in his dementia, Jefferson clarified. Everyone knows and everyone is here waiting to see you."

"Even Gus?" Dark brows lifted in disbelief.

"*Especially* Gus. He's hoping you can forgive him. I've taken the liberty of suggesting that you will. If I've overstepped, I'm sorry."

Adams smiled ruefully. "He's an ornery old cuss. Always has been, always will be. But I love him. I suppose I always will."

That was the consensus of most everyone at the party. Though none were privy to the concerns of Adams' return, it was enough that he'd come, that he'd labored alongside his brothers to save a home he'd been denied. All for a man who had rejected him when he needed a father most. That was their proof.

"Gus Cade is fortunate in his sons." Tears threatening, Eden spoke the opinion of most of Belle Terre.

"Maybe." Adams recalled the rare tender times, the times Gus dared show his emotions. He was a proud and hard man, but Adams understood at last that he truly cared. "Anyway, our children need one grandparent at least. Even a curmudgeon."

Reaching up with his good arm, he tangled his fingers in Eden's hair. "Maybe we'll have a little girl who will wrap herself around his heart like her mother did mine so long ago."

Eden cringed. To love Adams and have his children was what she'd wanted most. But there was something she had to tell him first, something she dreaded telling him. "Adams," she said hesitantly, "when we made love on the beach, you asked if I was protected."

Adams watched her intently. "You said yes."

She looked away, unable to hold his gaze. "That wasn't quite the truth. I had no protection."

"Because you've been told it's highly unlikely you could ever conceive a child. Cullen told me. Our silent islander can be quite talkative with a bottle of wine under his belt."

"Cullen?" Eden was astonished. He never discussed private matters. With anyone. "When did he tell you?"

"Just before I left the river cottage. He arrived at my door with a couple of bottles of wine, invited himself in and proceeded to demand that I tell him what my intentions were toward you. In the course of the conversation he vowed that if I hurt you, he'd kill me. Then he told me you'd been hurt enough, and why.

"I know that Nicholas Claibourne had an inherited degenerative disease he wanted to stop with him. I know he was so fearful you would conceive his child that measures were taken to see it wouldn't happen. Then it was discovered there was little chance of it due to a minor physical anomaly. An anomaly that can be corrected, sweetheart,'' he said quietly. ''If you wish.''

''Cullen told you all this? I didn't realize he knew.''

''There was more.'' With a tug he drew her to his kiss. ''I know Nicholas Claibourne was a man of little passion, and though you loved him, he didn't care that you loved me more.''

''Nicholas knew from the beginning that you were first in my heart. That you would always be,'' Eden admitted. ''It was part of the attraction. He didn't have long to live, and he knew it.

''The last thing he wanted was that I love him so deeply I would want to have his child. He wanted no part of him left. No child to inherit and perpetuate his terrible legacy.

''I understood from the start that Nicholas wanted a friend more than a wife. Even so, our marriage was good, Adams.''

''None of that matters,'' he said softly. ''We're free of our pasts and finally together. I'd like it to be that way forever.''

''But if this…anomaly can't be corrected?'' Her heart stood still in fear that, no matter how much he loved her, he wouldn't want her if she couldn't give him children.

''Ah, my Eden.'' Adams smiled. ''There are children all over the world who need someone. We make them ours by loving them.

''Now, I'm tired. I need to sleep, and I want to sleep with you. Just you. No hospital gown, nothing but your skin against mine. As it was on Summer Island.''

''Your arm. I might hurt you,'' she whispered.

''Not as much as not holding you. We'll manage, Eden. Whatever happens, now or in the future.''

''Yes,'' Eden promised as her heart soared, ''we will.''

Stripped to a G-string, she lay with her body curved

into his. His hand wandered to the ribbons at her hip. "One day," he said, "I'd like to sleep with you on the beach where you sunbathe like this."

"All we'll need is a boat and a blanket," she promised.

"And a little more stamina," Adams suggested.

"What about Gus?"

"You want Gus to go to the island with us?" Adams' voice was heavy with tongue-in-cheek humor as fatigue descended.

"No, silly. He's waiting outside to see you."

"He's kept me waiting thirteen years. Another day won't hurt." Adams kissed the back of her neck wishing he had the strength for more than a kiss.

"Adams?" Eden's mind was hopscotching.

"Another question, love?"

"How did you know Jefferson had gone to Rabb Town?"

"I didn't. I missed his horse and saddle when I checked the barn before turning in. Jeffie was gone, but I didn't know where. I trailed him awhile. Then I knew." A bitter note crept into his slurring voice. "I should have known from the first."

"Why?" Eden laced her fingers through his good hand and brought it to her naked breast. "Why should you have known?"

Adams caught a long breath and found comfort in the softness of her body. "Junior hated me. More for being a Cade than for any other reason. He said some things in town that morning. The usual hate-filled garbage. I laughed it off, but Jeffie decided he should redeem my honor."

"Then he went to Rabb Town for you. Because he did, you count all that happened as your fault."

"That's part of it," Adams admitted. "And Gus."

"Yes," Eden whispered. "And Gus."

With that she fell silent, consumed by her thoughts. Once, Adams had been her champion, then Jefferson's. And now again. How fortunate they were to have Adams. How fortunate for all of them. Even Gus Cade. Especially Gus Cade.

Hurrying footsteps sounded in the hall as the nursing staff readied patients for bed. None paused at Adams' door. None dared. If the sign instructing that the occupants were not to be disturbed hadn't been deterrent enough, the big islander who stood guard would have.

"Adams." Eden's voice was drowsy. "I love you."

Smiling, Adams held her tighter. Closing her eyes, savoring the beat of his heart and the touch of his body, Eden slept in her lover's arms.

The room was quiet when the door opened and Cullen looked in. Eden Roberts Claibourne was finally where she belonged.

There were legal details to work out. But with Lincoln and Jackson and Jefferson helping, Jericho had already begun unsnarling the silence of years. When the truth that each brother had saved the life of the other was finally public knowledge, it would all be set right. Then the world would know that the man who held Eden in his arms was a good son, a good brother, a man of great strength and greater honor.

Then Belle Terre could truly celebrate the return of Adams Cade. But the true celebration was that of two lovers, as deep in the night, Adams stirred and awoke, and whispered against her hair the words he'd carried in his heart for years, "I love you, Eden. I have loved you through all our yesterdays. I will love you tomorrow and tomorrow and—"

"Forever," she finished for him, making her own

pledge, giving irrevocably into his care the heart he'd won so long ago.

"Forever," Adams Cade, once the hardened outcast who thought he'd lost the gentleness and joy of loving, repeated softly, "and ever."

* * * * *

Don't miss the next powerful
story in BJ James' new series

MEN OF BELLE TERRE

coming in December 2000
only from Silhouette Desire.

July 2000
BACHELOR DOCTOR
#1303 by Barbara Boswell

August 2000
THE RETURN OF ADAMS CADE
#1309 by BJ James
Men of Belle Terre

September 2000
SLOW WALTZ ACROSS TEXAS
#1315 by Peggy Moreland
Texas Grooms

October 2000
THE DAKOTA MAN
#1321 by Joan Hohl

November 2000
HER PERFECT MAN
#1328 by Mary Lynn Baxter

December 2000
IRRESISTIBLE YOU
#1333 by Barbara Boswell

MAN OF THE MONTH

For twenty years Silhouette has been giving
you the ultimate in romantic reads. Come join
some of your favorite authors in helping us to
celebrate our anniversary with the most rugged,
sexy and lovable heroes ever!

Available at your favorite retail outlet.

Silhouette®

Where love comes alive™

**Don't miss
an exciting opportunity
to save on the purchase of
Harlequin and Silhouette books!**

Buy any two Harlequin or
Silhouette books and save
$10.00 off future Harlequin
and Silhouette purchases

OR

buy any three
Harlequin or Silhouette books
and save **$20.00 off** future
Harlequin and Silhouette purchases.

**Watch for details
coming in October 2000!**

PHQ400

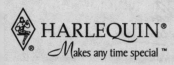

If you enjoyed what you just read,
then we've got an offer you can't resist!

Take 2 bestselling love stories FREE!

Plus get a FREE surprise gift!

Clip this page and mail it to Silhouette Reader Service™

IN U.S.A.	IN CANADA
3010 Walden Ave.	P.O. Box 609
P.O. Box 1867	Fort Erie, Ontario
Buffalo, N.Y. 14240-1867	L2A 5X3

YES! Please send me 2 free Silhouette Desire® novels and my free surprise gift. Then send me 6 brand-new novels every month, which I will receive months before they're available in stores. In the U.S.A., bill me at the bargain price of $3.34 plus 25¢ delivery per book and applicable sales tax, if any*. In Canada, bill me at the bargain price of $3.74 plus 25¢ delivery per book and applicable taxes**. That's the complete price and a savings of at least 10% off the cover prices—what a great deal! I understand that accepting the 2 free books and gift places me under no obligation ever to buy any books. I can always return a shipment and cancel at any time. Even if I never buy another book from Silhouette, the 2 free books and gift are mine to keep forever. So why not take us up on our invitation. You'll be glad you did!

225 SEN C222

326 SEN C223

Name	(PLEASE PRINT)	
Address	Apt.#	
City	State/Prov.	Zip/Postal Code

* Terms and prices subject to change without notice. Sales tax applicable in N.Y.

** Canadian residents will be charged applicable provincial taxes and GST.

All orders subject to approval. Offer limited to one per household.

® are registered trademarks of Harlequin Enterprises Limited.

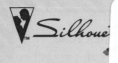

COMING NEXT MONTH